MURDER IS

MATERIAL

A BRIGID DONOVAN MYSTERY

KAREN SAUM

New Victoria Publishers

Published by New Victoria Publishers Inc., a feminist, literary, and cultural organization, PO Box 27, Norwich, VT 05055-0027.

Cover design by Ginger Brown

First printing.
Printed on recycled paper in the United States of America
1 2 3 4 5   1997   1996   1995   1994

Library of Congress Cataloging-in-Publication Data
Saum, Karen, 1935-
   Murder is material : a Brigid Donovan mystery / by Karen Saum.
     p. cm.
   ISBN 0-934678-57-X : $9.95
PS3569.A7887M865 1994
813' .54-- dc20   94-15389
                                              CIP

For Anne Bishop and Jan Morrill whose kind hospitality made
Brigid's adventures in Halifax possible.

Chapter 1

"Brigid, you're in love with this Sister Pat you keep visiting, and the reason is: You feel safe with her. Her being a nun, and all, and having this partner, Sister Barnabas, you hate so much. Brigid, get a life!"

That advice, given to me at a meeting a while back is true, I guess, in a way—at least that part about needing to get a life. A recovering alcoholic—and working the program—I don't have much time to go dancing. That's what I tell myself. The trouble I get myself into, though, is beyond belief. Like the matter with Julie. I might do better going to a party now and then.

Over the years here in Maine, I've built a small reputation as someone who can unravel mysteries. It all started shortly after I got sober. To while away long winter evenings, I investigated an ancient unsolved murder in the Allagash and identified the perpetrator. To while away my second sober winter I wrote about it.

In my other life, before AA, mistaking a school girl crush for a vocation, I entered a convent. My first attempt at recovery was to recover from an overdose of theology. For a bridegroom I exchanged Jesus for someone who only thought he was. Or so it seemed at the time. I had by then become wedded to the bottle. The twins happened in there somewhere, and, after my divorce, Heidi McCarren, the twins' other mother. When I moved to Maine, I figured I had enough memories to last me through retirement, since mostly I didn't want to think about them, anyway. Sister Pat I met during my first real murder investigation. By then I was able to distinguish infatuation from calling; it wasn't so clear to me, however, that Pat could.

In any case, I didn't follow the advice to get a life. Instead, I let Sister Pat talk me into building myself a shed at 'The Cloisters,' the misleading name she christened the bedraggled convent/farm she homesteads with Sister Barnabas, her black-mailing partner in Christ. That's how I came to meet Julie and become entangled in the affairs of the Compton family.

When I stay at the Cloisters, Sister Pat sticks me into the cell next to hers. She thinks I stay because I like her bread. The real reason is the flimsy construction. All night long I hear her moving around, sighing sometimes. In the morning I hear her stretch, listen while she burrows again into her pillow, hear the clicking noises she makes with her tongue, right next to my ear, because when she starts to wake up, I scrunch up close to the rough pine boarding that separates us. It's practically like being in bed with her. I think.

Then I lie quietly until I smell the coffee. Usually we have our first cup together in a companionable silence while Barney sleeps. But not this one morning, the morning I met Julie.

When I reached the living room, Barney, in her habit, was already at the table, a white candle casting pale light on the open Lectionary, bright red and gold, before her. Next to her sat a wisp of fair hair and gauzy draperies, like a little girl acting grown-up in company, the enveloping shawls and lace mantilla taken from her "dress-up box." The person held her hands clasped penitentially before her. Pat wasn't there.

"You missed the service," said Barney reprovingly, her mouth screwed hard as a nut. I noticed she looked her age, even in candle light. At sixty-one, Barney's only a few years older than I.

"It's only six," I said defensively. In my pajamas, I felt at a disadvantage. But Barney usually has that effect on me, even when I'm dressed in boots, chainsaw in hand. Legacy of parochial schools and time served in a convent of my own when I was too young to know better.

"I guess," said Barney, spitting out the words like poisoned pellets, "Pat failed to tell you."

"Tell me what?"

Barney gestured deferentially to the fey creature at her side. "Brigid, I would like you to meet Julie."

I rubbed my eyes. Barney, the old bat, was actually simpering.

"Hi," I said. Julie nodded shyly, her eyes slipping under the table.

"Is there coffee?" I asked.

"You perhaps have heard of Julie," said Barney, stern as usual addressing me.

I hadn't. I said, "Hmm." Then I said "Hi!" again. "Um, what happened to the coffee?"

"The stigmata?" Barney said.

"The stigmata?" I repeated stupidly.

"Show her " Barney commanded.

From beneath the layers of filmy material, small white-gloved hands rose and turned for my inspection. Staining the palms were drops of blood, some fresh and scarlet breaking through the brown crust of blood that had dried and darkened.

As I stared, the girl raised her head. My eyes met hers, pale blue and serene. The lace of her mantilla touched her brows, obscuring the pale high forehead and soft blond hair. She looked like a Renaissance Madonna, a Leonardo, perhaps, looking up from the babes at play, Jesus and John. Her hands lay placidly in mine, the passive fingers curled as if to bless. Blood welled in the palm of one. The curve of her nostrils, the plump fullness of her mouth reminded me of a Botticelli. I wondered what torment found its sole expression in those subtle curves. I thought of Genevieve, another troubled Religious I had met a few years before here at the Cloisters.

"You should put some A&D ointment on those," I said. returning her hands to her. A look like alarm flitted across the surface of her eyes.

"Scoff!" Barney invited.

"Hey," I murmured, "all I want is a cup of coffee."

While I puttered at the sink, a long slate trough with a little red hand-pump at one end, Barney read some letters of Paul to various sectarians in the Middle East, long shopping lists of "dos" and "don'ts", mostly "don'ts." I decided, half listening, that in his seminarian days Stalin must have read a lot of Paul. I took my cup of coffee when it was brewed and started with it up the ladder to the loft. Barney stopped me.

"Julie came to talk with you, Brigid. Perhaps you could spare her a minute? She needs help. Pat suggested your name."

My name? I thought. But I stayed cool.

"Yeah," I said. "Let me get dressed, okay?"

Julie, when I returned, was seated in an armchair under St. Joseph, baby Jesus in his arms. I didn't see Barney.

Responding to my glance around the room, Julie said, "She's gone."

Her voice surprised me. Clear and cool. Light from the window, more revealing than candlelight, showed that she was a woman not a girl, in her early twenties perhaps. A woman, I thought, with troubles. Between her brows, worry lines had begun to form. I felt a momentary pang for the way I had dismissed her bloodied palms.

"What can I do for you?" I asked.

"You don't like me," she began.

To myself I said the Serenity Prayer. "God grant me the serenity to accept the things I cannot change." Then, for good measure, called on my Guardian Angel. I must have been staring out-of-focus at Joseph, for Julie interrupted, saying, "Hello? You there?"

"Yeah. You were saying?"

"Barney told me you could help me."

"She did?"

Her grandmother. Julie serenely asserted, intended to murder her. This I found about as believable as her stigmata. I said, ."Oh yeah?"

"See," she said, "I told Barney you wouldn't believe me."

Guardian Angel and I had another little chat. This time Julie sat through it in silence.

"Who's your grandmother?" I asked after a while.

Her grandmother was Pearl MacDonald, Director of H.O.P.E., an ecumenical group providing a range of services from shelters for the homeless to counseling for the disturbed. The acronym stood for Helping Others, the Poor Especially. MacDonald, I knew, had been Director for only three years, but in that time she had transformed the place. From a sleepy little cluster of buildings and pasture within the hamlet of Surry, Maine, H.O.P.E. had become a bustling center of economic activity larger than Surry itself.

Rumor had it that two similar groups recently organized in Washington County and Waldo were, in fact, owned by H.O.P.E.

"She's not like people think, you know, like Mother Theresa and stuff, she's not like that."

"She's not? What is she like?"

"She's a fucking bitch, if you want to know the truth," said Julie.

"Tell me about it," I invited, wondering, briefly, whether those fifteenth century models for angels and saints had talked dirty too, out on the streets after work. Probably they had.

"Well, for one thing," Julie said, "she's jealous. You know, of me, because of Arjuna and, like, the stigmata and stuff."

Arjuna. I knew the name. Like Rajneesh, who had taken coastal Maine by storm in the seventies, Arjuna preached a user-friendly Buddhism that had won converts in back-to-the-landers who had failed to find salvation in wood-burning stoves and organically grown herbs.

"What has Arjuna got to do with the stigmata," I asked diffidently, reluctant, really, to get into it.

Julie moved restlessly and looked reproachful. She raised her palms toward me. She might have been warding off a blow. "Don't you know?" she said. "He and I live together at my grandmother's place. H.O.P.E." She said the word scornfully.

"I see," I said, not sure that I did. Finally I asked, "You say your grandmother's jealous. Jealous like envy? Or jealous like 'in love' and jealous?"

Julie looked perplexed. Perhaps such fine distinctions puzzled her. She opted, with a sigh, not to choose. "She's envious all right. But she's jealous, too."

"Are you and Arjuna lovers, then?"

5

"Arjuna?" she sneered. "He's old enough to be my grandfather!"

"You didn't answer my question."

"So what if we are?"

"So, Pearl MacDonald's in love with Arjuna and envies you because you have the stigmata."

"I knew you wouldn't believe me."

"Tell me some more about Arjuna."

I'll leave out most of her reply, a string of superlatives, like, I mean, the greatest. I tried unsuccessfully, as I watched her lovely lips at work, to imagine La Giaconda, when she isn't busy with her Mona Lisa smile, uttering similar banalities.

The kernel of Julie's response was that Arjuna was behind an effort to build a Buddhist temple and condominium complex in Soperton, the hamlet where Sister Pat's farm is situated. Julie's grandmother, Pearl MacDonald, was trying to sabotage the project. This because Pearl saw in Arjuna a rival huckster purveying a new line of spiritual goods in an inelastic market. My words.

In her agitation Julie had begun to pace back and forth between the cookstove and St. Joseph,. netting, like blowing bubbles, floated behind her.

"Where does the stigmata come in?" I asked.

"Whatta ya mean 'come in'?" She stopped in front of me and thrust her hands in my face. The bleeding had stopped. The palms of the bright white gloves appeared simply dirty. I looked away.

"Nothing disparaging. It just seems odd. When I think of stigmata I think of St. Francis, I think of Catholicism."

"Snows how much you know," she said and flounced down in the chair again. "Great Religious through the ages have displayed Stigmata," she quoted someone,.Arjuna maybe.

I said, mildly I hoped, "And you're a Great Religious?"

"*Arjuna.* You don't get it do you?"

"I guess not."

"See, Pearl, she's used to things going her way, then this guru comes along and where's she at? I mean, next to Arjuna who's Pearl MacDonald?"

Julie didn't wait for an answer. "Nobody, that's who. And then what happens? Her own granddaughter like starts seeing this person she only thinks of as a rival, you know, because of her limited karma. Then I go and get the stigmata! Trust me, she wants me out of the way."

"You have it here too?" I gestured under my arm.

"No, just these."

"Does it hurt?"

"A little. Not bad."

She sounded to me like a carnival barker, or worse: a shill. Like asking a fire eater, do the flames burn, and she says, "Not once you get used to it." I wished again I could take her more seriously.

"So what do you want me to do?"

"Investigate her."

"Investigate her."

"Yeah. Like let her know you're on her case. That way she'll like be afraid to step out of line. Barney says you're a wizard," she added hopefully.

"Wizard?"

"God!" she sighed. "You know, like good."

"Okay."

She looked surprised. "Just like that? Okay?"

"Why not? I charge $100 a day plus expenses."

"You serious?"

"Never more so."

"Okay." A smile fluttered the Renaissance ripeness of her mouth.

I regretted my words immediately. Julie was more than a little schizophrenic and it was wrong to play with her. Worse than wrong, stupid. The stigmata, like believing one is Christ, is garden variety paranoia and probably not too dangerous. Believing someone wants to kill you is more problematic. There was also the possibility Julie was just training to be a con. Whatever, there was a pathetic quality to her loveliness and I responded to it. I wasn't the only one.

Barney walked in and smiled at me expectantly. I realized I

had been snookered. I didn't know why, but I was certain it was Barney who wanted me to investigate Julie's grandmother Pearl MacDonald. She's used Julie to bait the trap, knowing I wouldn't tell her the time of day if she asked.

"Have you two settled everything?" asked Barney, sweetly as she was able.

Chapter 2

Mid-morning I drove over to H.O.P.E. But first, after break-fast, I looked for Pat. I found her out back singing to Rosie, the goat she milks for making cheese. Chevron, rather. The difference, Pat told me, between goats milk cheese and chevron is about three dollars a pound. As chevron, Barney peddles it to a couple of gourmet shops and several restaurants along the coast. It's good, especially the kind Pat adds herbs to.

"Barney talk you into helping Julie?" asked Pat, avoiding my eyes.

Barney doesn't ask people to do things by saying, "Please would you." She tries to blackmail them instead. Like the time when we first met and she threatened to tell the world I was a dyke unless I helped build the Kingdom of God for her. The particular building she had in mind was a road into the Cloisters. I didn't have any money, and I'd already told the world, so it didn't work. But that's what I dislike about Barney, not that she's Pat's partner. I think.

I didn't answer Pat right away. I enjoyed just looking at her. Enjoyed her discomfort a little, too, I guess. She won't believe me about Barney. Pat was dressed in jeans and a flannel shirt, as she usually was these days. When I first met her, chasing Charley, an escaping pig, she wore her habit even doing chores. The coif would hide her hair, abundant and red. That morning a bandan-na hid it, most of it anyway. What I could see was bright orange, recently hennaed.

"Yeah, she did," I said finally, rubbing Rosie where her horns had budded.

Turning her head into Rosie's flank, Pat energetically squeezed several thin streams of milk before replying. Then all she did was mutter, "I thought you'd be angry."

I laughed. "I talked myself into it," I said and described my conversation with Julie. "You ever meet this Arjuna?" I asked. Then, "What's with the name? He Indian?"

"Indian!" Pat snorted.

Arjuna, Pat said, was about as Indian as her Aunt Nelly, and, like her, had grown up in one of the Atlantic Provinces of Canada. What made her so curt, Pat eventually explained, was "the hypocrisy of it all."

We had moved to the hen house which she began to muck out with a long-tined pitchfork. I took the fork from her saying if she would talk, I would muck. "Why not?" she agreed.

Arjuna had arrived in Maine at the beginning of the year preaching godliness: Asceticism, humility and love. The brotherly kind of love. He had quickly picked up a following among the big city refugees who had flocked to Maine in the sixties and seventies. Those with money, that is. "He charges ten dollars a head to watch him sit cross-legged on a pillow and ramble a while," said Pat. Her informant, she said, was Barney.

"Barney went to hear Arjuna?" I asked, incredulous.

Pat looked embarrassed again and wouldn't meet my eyes. The plot, I thought, was thickening. Maybe Barney wanted me to look into Julie's allegations against Pearl in order to find out something she could use to blackmail Arjuna. That made sense to me: If Arjuna collected ten dollars a head from people wanting to watch him sit cross-legged and ramble, he probably had walking-around money to support the Cloisters for years.

"I'll take over if you like," said Pat, reaching for the fork. She stood just outside the door of the coop. A beam of sunlight played in her hair. There's a little mole down along her jaw. The copper hairs there glinted in the light.

"That's okay," I said. I caught her hand, but she withdrew it.

Hastily. "Keep talking," I said and bent again to my labors.

She said there wasn't much to tell. Besides rumors. Then she said Rajneesh might have been disgusting, but at least he was honest.

Rajneesh, preaching free love for salvation during the seventies, picked up followers in Maine like a dog picks up fleas. Some people saw the heart of Maine's real estate boom in the Rajneesh craze.

The problem, as Pat saw it, with Arjuna was that he preached one thing and did another.

"You mean the affair with Julie?"

"That," she said, "is small beer."

"Oh yeah?" I said, inviting more information. She looked so uncomfortable I realized suddenly what a long draft would be. "He likes boys?" I asked.

Pat swept off her bandanna. Her hair bounded, brassy, into the sunlight. Like Sampson, I thought. But she didn't answer my question. Pat tries not to speak ill of others. I tried another tack. "Julie says her grandmother is going to murder her."

"Poor Julie," Pat murmured.

"You like her?"

"Don't," Pat warned, "judge her too harshly."

I asked what she made of Julie's stigmata. Pat brushed away the stigmata. She said, "Oh that."

"Does anyone believe it?"

"Does anyone believe Medjugorje?" she asked, referring to the town in what was once Yugoslavia where children reported seeing the Virgin Mary, and thousands still risk their lives to check it out.

"What do you think of Pearl MacDonald?" I asked next.

"The Milken of East Surry?"

"She's an inside trader?" I asked, puzzled.

"A wheeler dealer," Pat said. "And I have to stop this conversation. I shouldn't talk this way about people. Why I joined a cloistered order. Some cloister." She laughed ruefully gazing around at the mud.

I can never decide what about Pat I love most: that she hennas her hair, or her transcendent optimism regarding the Cloisters.

At H.O.P.E. I was in luck. MacDonald was in and had a few minutes to spare. I wondered whether Barney had arranged it.

"Pearl MacDonald," she said. "And you're Brigid Donovan? How can I help you?"

She stood up from her desk to greet me, reaching over mountains of papers, books and tackle to grasp my hand in a hearty shake. Her appearance surprised me. I must have expected something more dynamic, or more holy. Like everyone else Downeast, she wore jeans and a flannel shirt. She looked her age, about sixty, her hair cropped short and gray, her eyes beginning to lose themselves in the bonier structures of her face. Glasses hung from her neck on twine. If she didn't resemble Mother Theresa or Leona Helmsley, neither did she look as if she planned to murder anyone. Least of all her granddaughter.

She gestured for me to sit, then laughed. Both chairs were piled high, like her desk, with paraphernalia. "Just knock it on the floor," she suggested.

I hadn't appreciated, when I agreed to come, just how awkward it would be. I took my time making room for myself on the chair. The minute I spent fussing seemed to have tried Pearl's patience. Her smile of welcome was pinched and fading fast. "Just throw that stuff on the floor," she said again.

"You've made a lot of improvements here," I began. "The new barn, and stuff." I began to tell her that I once had written a history of H.O.P.E. She stopped me.

"I've read your history. It's very good," she added. "I don't want to hurry you, but I have a ten o'clock appointment in Machias."

I glanced at my watch. "You'll be late," I said. I had an inspiration. "Let me drive you."

It was ten-fifteen by the time we entered Machias, the frost heaves having kept me to an average speed of about thirty miles an hour. I dropped Pearl on Main Street at the Pine Tree Legal Assistance offices where her appointment was. We agreed to meet later at Helen's. She said the walk would do her good.

Except for her impatience when I slowed for heaves, Pearl had been friendly enough on the drive. And she had spoken easily about herself, about her childhood in Pictou County, Nova Scotia. Being orphaned and brought up by "the Sisters." Unlike myself, Pearl had never confused her emotions for a calling. I had mistaken falling in love with my high school history teacher, Sister Anne, with wanting to be a bride of Christ. I entered the convent when I was seventeen. Having acted in haste, I repented at leisure, repented through my novitiate, and then, after leaving the convent, did penance through a miserable marriage.

Pearl, on the other hand, went from the convent school to St. Francis Xavier in Antigonish, and there became a student of Coady International Institute. As a Coady graduate, in the early fifties, she had gone to work in India.

"I thought Julie was your granddaughter," I said, unable to fit a marriage and family into this busy life.

"Oh, she is." After an uncomfortable silence, Pearl added, "I was sixteen."

"I didn't mean to pry," I lied, embarrassed.

Pearl sighed. "No problem," she said. Then, "It was rape. The Sisters took the baby. Another reason to be grateful to them."

"You kept in touch?" I ventured.

"Not with him. Not then. But with the Sisters, of course."

We drove a while in silence, through Milbridge and Harrington, each of us busy with her own thoughts. Later, up on the blueberry barrens outside Columbia Falls, the spring fields like fire, brilliant red and orange in the sun, she took up her story again. "The Sisters were good to Eddie. Helped him get a scholarship to Dalhousie. Afterwards he went to Pratt, in New York. Got his degree in architecture."

"Eddie MacDonald! He's your son?"

She nodded. A pleased smile played on her lips, well formed, but thin, quite unlike the sensual fullness of her granddaughter Julie's mouth.

Eddie MacDonald had made the *Maine Times* on a couple of occasions for his architectural projects. The Buddhist temple

13

coming to Soperton had been designed by him.

"What do you think," I asked Pearl, "about this Buddhist temple they're going to build? Julie says you're not too pleased."

"Poor Julie," Pearl sighed, much as Pat had done.

"Julie seems to think you're afraid of the competition," I said, drawing up to the curb outside *Your Store*, the Machias food CO-OP.

"Is that what you came to see me about?" She turned to face me squarely. Close like that I could see her eyes clearly. They were dark and bright, like chips of mica set in granite.

"Yes," I admitted.

"When I get to Helen's, we can discuss it over lunch."

It was a little after twelve when she arrived, looking pleased with herself. "Things go well?" I asked.

Rubbing the palms of her hands together, contemplating the menu, Pearl said, "I guess things went well! If you call making five hundred acres of idle land available for the poor 'going well'. I think I'll have their seafood chowder."

Pearl told me 'poor' Julie couldn't be more mistaken than to think she was afraid of Arjuna's competition. "Any good fund raiser will tell you," she said, "the more the merrier. Whoever heard of Soperton, Maine, even eighteen months ago? Now people plan their vacations around seeing it. What there is to see," she added.

"No, what Julie calls competition is like sowing the crop. Every car that passes through Surry drops, on average, nearly sixty dollars at H.O.P.E.'s craft store. Fifty-eight forty-nine to be exact. We've kept records since my coming. Multiply that by a thousand and what do you get? We're planning to open a new store in Soperton when they start to lay the foundation of the temple."

I worked it out. If you believed her—and it was hard not to, her presentation, even though she ate clam chowder making it, had a crisp authority—if you believed her, each thousand cars meant over fifty-eight thousand dollars into the little craft store at H.O.P.E. That spelled big boon to the local economy, of the poor community especially.

"What about the sub-division they want to build?" I asked. "Is that good too?"

14

"Depends. Depends on what people want and what they're willing to fight for. I have a ratio: For every second home built, one home for the homeless. That translates, in Soperton, for every condo, one family farm. They want two hundred acres for two hundred condos? Fine, we want a thousand acres for two hundred family farms. But," she winked, "we'll settle for five hundred acres plus capital to build two homes. That way we can keep turning the money over as the homes are built and mortgaged."

She looked ready for dessert, dessert then dragons. Two hours ago she'd seemed non-descript. Now she resembled St. George, a flush of color on the high neat bones of her cheeks, her eyes bright with visions of battles past and battles yet to come. I got the feeling that her banner was less important to her than the campaigns she waged under it.

I recommended the graham cracker pie. She ordered banana cream. I said, "So, Julie's all wet."

"Poor Julie," she murmured again.

"What do you think of Arjuna?" I asked.

"What's to think? He's good at what he does."

"And that's?"

"If you have ten dollars to spare, find out for yourself," she invited.

"You don't like him."

"Brigid, I try my damnedest to love everyone, *caritas*. But very few people I like. And Arjuna is not one of them. My work," she said. "I like that."

We decided to go home by way of Tunk Lake. It was too cold to swim, but Pearl suggested that we stop and test the water. The woods were tinged chartreuse and rose, and popple had begun to leaf. One more day of warm weather, the black flies would be out.

While we dried our feet with our socks, Pearl confided that Barney had warned her of my visit. "She said you'd agreed to investigate me for Julie."

She seemed amused. I busied myself between my toes.

"If you intend to earn that hundred dollars a day, you should really go to Nova Scotia and visit the Sisters of Sainte Therese. The orphanage. I grew up there."

I continued to dry my toes, inspecting them one by one for signs of moisture.

"You should visit St. F. X., too. In Antigonish. You know, the Coady Institute at St. Francis Xavier."

I grudged her a "Yeah."

"You'll go?"

I turned and faced her. She'd bagged five hundred acres of land that morning. I wondered what she was hunting now. "Maybe," I said. "Why?"

"Well, if you do go, I'd like to hire you to do a job for me. I have a van load of stuff—clothing, household appliances, some can goods and furniture—I'd like you to take them to Cape Breton for me. Just another fifty miles or so beyond Antigonish. An Indian reservation there. Eskasoni."

"Hire?"

She laughed. "I can't afford a hundred a day, but yes, hire. How does eighty dollars for the trip sound?"

"It sounds good. But when I knew H.O.P.E. it was a poor people's organization. 'Live simply so others can simply live.'" I quoted the motto I used in the preface of the history I had written. "People mostly volunteered."

"Would you rather volunteer?"

I thought about it. The question had been a challenge, and I wanted to confound her expectations. Also, I needed not to have her laugh at me. I couldn't think whether what I really wanted was to volunteer or to be paid. I managed to center myself with what Julie might call a mantra: "God grant me the serenity to accept the things I cannot change."

I realized I didn't want her money. And I didn't want to play her games. "You don't need to pay me."

"Good. It's done then. The van will be ready tomorrow."

Passing through Franklin, she confided that a foundation was sending the contributions to Cape Breton. "They pay twenty-five cents a mile," she said, staring at my profile.

I don't think I gratified her. Some deep breathing kept me jolly. The excess oxygen probably.

Figuring a thousand miles to Cape Breton and back, that

made two hundred fifty dollars for travel. "Must be gold plated, those appliances," I said.

"Junk, mostly," she replied. "Tax write-offs. That's where the money is."

I seemed to have entered the world of high finance charity.

"Don't worry," Pearl laughed. "I intend to pay you."

The rest of the way home we were both silent. Pearl slaying dragons. Me trying to slay my doubts.

It puzzled me that Barney had called to warn Pearl of my visit. But then, I reflected, Julie had said all she really wanted was to make Pearl pause, to realize that it wouldn't be safe to mess with her granddaughter. I was reluctant even to think the word 'murder' it seemed so bizarre.

But why would Pearl practically act as tour guide to my inspection of her life? And pay for my ticket, to boot. Maybe because she was innocent and wanted to get this intrusion over with. Or maybe, I realized, because she thought she could control the spin if she knew beforehand what I was apt to report.

And I couldn't help wondering what was in it for Barney. There was the new opulence at H.O.P.E.. Had the Church entered the picture. Did Barney hope to blackmail Pearl into a soft sinecure there?

I liked that idea. The Cloisters without Barney was my idea of Heaven after Purgatory.

Chapter 3

Pearl had arranged for me to stop at St. Therese, the orphanage outside Halifax where she had spent her childhood. "You can stay the night, investigate me, and pick up some more stuff for Eskasoni," she said.

She paid up front for the job: five Andrew Jacksons so crisp and new they stuck together.

"One too many," I said, trying, after I'd managed to pry it loose, to hand the last one back.

"Keep it," she said, amused. "Arjuna's playing at the University tomorrow. Go see him. Take a friend."

Back at the Cloisters that night I tried to talk Sister Pat into going with me. Turned out to be a waste of effort.

Next morning I was awakened not by Pat's soft rustles, but by a great tumult downstairs. A high pitched keening. I knew, before my feet hit the floor, that someone had died.

Julie of the many veils stood in the kitchen shrieking and bleeding. Her cheeks, raked by her nails, ran with blood. Barney, in a flannel robe, rushed past me to take charge. She secured Julie's arms behind her and wrestled her into the armchair under St. Joseph's benevolent gaze.

"Don't just stand there," Barney panted, "throw some water on her."

Pat, climbing down the ladder behind me, pushed me to one

side. "Coming," she muttered, "coming."

A few minutes later a wetter but calmer Julie lay sobbing in Barney's arms. Pat found some brandy which Barney administered in a cup of coffee. And, as that took effect, Julie explained that Arjuna was dead.

"She murdered him!" Julie cried again and again.

"Why don't I call Edith," I said to Pat. "She has a police scanner."

The police report, according to our old friend, Edith, was that Arjuna had been killed an hour or so earlier.

"The victim, that's your friend Arjuna," said Edith, "died in the blaze. They aren't sure yet whether he died of smoke inhalation or was burned. I guess there wasn't much left of him. Did he smoke?" she asked.

"I don't know. Maybe. It's not arson, then?"

"Suspicious circumstances," said Edith. "What was suspicious they didn't say."

After relaying Edith's information to Pat, I asked, "Where did Arjuna live?"

"He and I live—I mean we lived at H.O.P.E.," Julie answered. "At Pearl's. Until the temple's finished. Pearl murdered him. I know she did."

Julie wept a while on Barney's breast. She raised her head appealingly, "All I could think of was to get away from there. I'm so scared of her."

Barney clucked a bit and stroked Julie's hair. Barney said things like "there, there" and "you did the right thing to come."

Julie began to hiccough. Just like any little girl with a runny nose and a tear-streaked face. The blood mingling with her tears might have been the cause of her grief rather than the result of it.

Barney continued to stroke her hair and make crooning noises. Pat, after the first flurry of excitement, had settled on a bench at the picnic table across the room. I went and sat beside her. It seemed prudent. Julie, for the first time, had touched me. Her grief had touched me, counterfeit though much of it seemed. Her hiccoughs were real. Real and pathetic. It was Barney's solicitude that had made me wary; but then, mistrusting Barney had become second nature to me.

"What should we do?" I whispered to Pat.

"We? You got a mouse in your pocket?" asked Pat tartly. "*I'm* going to make more coffee."

It wasn't easy to persuade Julie to return to the scene of the tragedy. But in the end Barney managed to convince her that she would sooner or later be forced to return, and that it would look better if she came on her own. I agreed to drive her there. She had, apparently, walked to the Cloisters from H.O.P.E..

It was only six, but the sun was up, had been for a while, and birds were in a frenzy, singing, courting, making nests and love. Julie seemed to have exhausted herself with grief, not to mention a four mile hike. She sat silent, huddled in the passenger seat of my old truck.

"How long you been living at H.O.P.E.?" I asked, thinking it might do her good to talk.

"H.O.P.E.!" she said contemptuously.

I think the word she muttered then was 'despair.' I hadn't suspected such linguistic talent.

I turned into H.O.P.E. and the road that led beyond, into the wooded hills and the community built by the well-intentioned volunteers who came to donate their time and labor.

Some wag had dubbed it 'Shangri-La,' someone who had endured a winter there in one of the so-called retreat houses hammered together with scraps of lumber and experienced nails.

It had been years since I had visited. Then, it was nothing but a muddy clearing in the woods, the several shacks like scabs on a running sore. My memory had not prepared me for the present reality. It really was a Shangri-La.

The rutted approach through the woods was the same, but as we rounded the last curve, I was astonished by the sight of well-fenced pastures, lush with new grass, where before there had been only boulders and broken fencing. Belgian draft horses, both gray and gold, and a couple of Morgans browsed contentedly. In the distance, where a lopsided one-story shed had housed an indiscriminate mixture of fowl, humans, and other animals, an imposing red barn towered.

"Wow! " I said.

A figure, emerging from the barn, waved us to a stop. In the crisp morning air, he wore, like an Arab, a short-sleeved burnoose that reached to his ankles. His feet were shod in sandals. His beard, curly and blond, like his hair, was silvered by frost, and when he spoke, his breath formed a cloud in the cold.

"Well, if it isn't Jesus," I remarked, slowing down to stop. H.O.P.E. had always attracted psychotic people. For one thing, the local loony bin kept discharging them with nowhere to go. The Sermon on the Mount, probably, is what prompted the Messiahs to take up residence there. "May my Father, God, bless you," the frosted figure said.

"Say what?" I replied, rolling down the window.

"Don't pay any attention to him," said Julie. "He's nuts." She leaned across me and shouted out the window, in his face, "Get lost, Arthur!"

Arthur put down his bucket of grain and made a large sign of the cross at us "Forgive them, Father, they know not what they do," he intoned. And then, in a startlingly different voice, he shrieked, "Jezebel! Wanton woman! Repent!"

I think he meant Julie, not me. She said, "Shut up, Arthur!" to him, and to me she muttered, "Come on, let's get out of here."

Julie explained as we drew away, that when he called her Mary or Mary Magdalen, she found it easy to get along with him. He was, she confided, fond of her. But then, she sighed, he'd get jealous and call her Jezebel. She was, she said, a little afraid of him then. "But I can handle, it," she assured me.

As we rounded the barn, the new Shangri-La appeared before us. There were no shacks. In the middle of a slight hollow or bowl that was the center of the community, stood a long, low building. Still raw with newness, it looked out of place, the architecture better suited for a tropical climate, a resort motel, perhaps. Two extended arms embraced a wide verandah and, of all things, a swimming pool. Trees had been planted, and shrubs. A manufactured 'rustic' fence supported rugosa roses interspersed with lilies, tulips and narcissus. "Jesus Christ!" I said. "What's happened to this place?"

"Pearl," Julie sighed. "Pearl happened to it."

I parked the truck in front. The central portion of the building was two stories high. There, Doric columns, Gothic tympanum and Renaissance windows achieved an odd harmony. For the first time I could understand why Julie and Arjuna might have wanted to live there. It was luxurious. And, besides, the price had maybe been right, Julie being Pearl's granddaughter, and, in spite of her denial, Pearl may really have been fond of Arjuna.

As I parked in front of the motel-like building, Julie turned mulish. She said, belligerently, that if I thought she was going to go in and see 'that murderess' I had a screw loose, so I left her, saying I'd be back in a minute and take her wherever she wanted to go.

Early as it was, the corridor inside throbbed with activity, people stiff-legged as marionettes opening and closing doors, nodding woodenly at one another and exchanging short words in whispers. It was the awkwardness of disaster for which they had learned no lines to say, no steps to dance. Some young thing Julie's age pointed me toward Pearl's office.

I thought for a moment the doorknob was a mammoth diamond. It wasn't. Just crystal, but gorgeous. The disorder of the office at H.O.P.E. was entirely missing here. The sleek teak desk that dominated the room was clear of papers and clutter. Pearl stood, her back to the door, gazing at a wall crowded with pictures. I recognized several: Martin Lather King, Jr., Mother Theresa, Pope John XXIII, Archbishop Oscar Romero. Coming closer, I saw she held one in her hands. It was of a youngish man, starting to bald, his beard long and curly, his oriental almond eyes bright with humor. Virile, rakish even. The eyes and bare chest made me think India, though Pearl had told me he was of European background.

"Arjuna?" I asked. I saw she had been crying. She only nodded and, fumbling, tried to rehang the picture.

"May I?" I asked, and took it from her. "This isn't recent."

Pearl seemed to have recovered. She said, briskly, "No. But he was in remarkably good shape. Too bad you never had a chance to meet him."

"I thought you disliked him," I probed.

"That's right," she said wryly, "I believe I wanted to murder him. Or was that Julie?"

I laughed. "Something like that. By the way, Julie's outside in my truck. She refused to come in. I think she shouldn't be alone. I don't know what to do with her," I added lamely.

"The police want to talk with her."

"Why's that?"

"She was—I think the phrase is," said Pearl, moving behind her polished desk and sitting down, "'the last person to see him alive.'"

"Oh. I didn't know. Actually, I don't know anything except that he was killed in a fire," I said.

Pearl accepted the invitation to enlighten me. She gestured for me to sit. I chose an arm chair across the room. What little she knew about the tragedy she had heard on the police scanner she said. But she could give me some background.

Arjuna and Julie had been staying in one of the new cottages built at Shangri-La for visiting luminaries of the contemporary peace and social justice firmament. The day before, in the afternoon, Arjuna had complained of a migraine. Pearl had fixed him a bromide, then Julie went with him to the cottage where she settled him in bed. The headaches lasted, Pearl said, for six to eight hours, so Julie had decided to spend the night in Pearl's office. Pearl gestured toward the Chippendale sofa between the windows.

"My rooms are at the end of the west wing. Julie's screams woke me. But by then it was too late to do anything."

Police, ambulance, and fire trucks converged on Shangri-La together. "It was three-thirty, quarter to four. Julie had disappeared." Pearl looked at me inquiringly.

"She came to us. It was about four when she got to the Cloisters. I don't know how she got there unless she walked."

"Julie? I doubt it. She probably got Jesus to drive her over."

"What?"

"You haven't met him?"

"You don't mean Arthur?"

"Arthur, Jesus. Julie calls him Arthur. She may be wise, though it annoys him. He has a motorbike and he adores Julie."

"Mary Magdalen?"

"I'm sure."

"On the scanner they called it arson."

"They don't know that. Are you certain?"

"Suspicious circumstances," I amended.

"Well, suspicious, of course. It's been warm, they've had no fires. The wiring is new, besides they had no lights on, no appliances. Arjuna doesn't smoke." She caught her breath, like a sob. "Didn't smoke."

Pearl opened a drawer, pulled out some tissues and blew her nose. "Take her into Ellsworth," she advised. "You know where the sheriff's office is? Take her there. I'll get Arthur to pick her up later this afternoon. Don't worry about her."

I found Julie, her draperies fluttering about her, beside the still smoldering ruins.

"Be careful," I warned, "you don't catch fire."

"I've thought about doing just that," she said sullenly. "I should, you know. I was married to him, really."

"Did Arjuna believe in suttee?" I asked to humor her.

"Of course not. He wasn't a Hindu," she said scornfully. I let it go.

"I'm taking you to Ellsworth," I told her.

"Why?"

"Sheriff wants to talk with you I guess."

"Good," she said. "I have a lot to tell him."

What Julie had to tell the sheriff she explained in detail as we made our way down Route 172 to Ellsworth. Arjuna had become fearful of Pearl and had decided to move out of Shangri-La. He had, in fact, decided to abandon the temple in Soperton. He wanted instead, to lead a new group in Nova Scotia. Cape Breton. If I didn't believe her, Julie said, I could just go and find out for myself. She claimed it was the tension with Pearl that had caused Arjuna's migraine headache.

"They had this big fight. Did Grandma tell you about that?"

"Pearl?"

"Yeah. Grandma. You old ladies don't like being called Grandma, do you?"

"I don't know about that. Pearl's not much like my Grandmother," I said mildly.

"Probably. Well, they had this monster fight and Arjuna got sick. Like he cannot deal with tension.

"He told Pearl we were leaving and stuff and she starts carrying on wicked. She like knew the only way to stop him was by doing what she did. You know, kill him. She poisoned him. Said it was for his headache." Julie snorted. "Bromide, she called it."

I said that was a pretty drastic solution. "Besides," I said, "Arjuna dead is Arjuna gone."

"Gone, yeah, but not with me. You don't get it. She was jealous. Not just envious. I told you."

She had. I guess it was one of the things I didn't believe. Didn't take seriously. I found it hard to take Julie seriously.

When I dropped her at the court house, I told her Arthur would be coming for her. She just grunted as she slid out the door. Then she turned and reached across the seat for my hand. Looking me earnestly in the eye, she said, "You'll get all the answers, you know, like in Nova Scotia." Then, pausing before she slammed the door, she said, "You don't believe me, but that is some dangerous lady. Just because Arjuna's dead, doesn't mean she still isn't planning to get rid of me. 'Cause she is!"

I laughed. A laugh I was shortly to regret.

Chapter 4

I picked Pearl's van up later that afternoon and started for Nova Scotia at sunrise next morning. Barney balked at paying me. Said hadn't Pearl paid me for the trip? Asked why I needed expenses, wasn't I staying at the convent? Was it my truck I was driving or Pearl's van? Said, finally, "Brigid, you used to care about the poor." Meaning, I guess, her.

A few twenty-four hours ago I was a rotten drunk. I still am. But, one day at a time, I don't take a drink, and over the years it's gotten easier. Barney's crack about not caring for the poor, meaning as it did, "You're a selfish bitch," would once have driven me to a drink. But not that day.

"A hundred a day plus expenses. Otherwise no investigation," I said.

Barney stood beside the black iron cookstove in the middle of the living area at the cloisters. She's close to six foot, and in her black and white, she could be Paul Bunyon as far as I was concerned. She brushed her hands together briskly. I wondered, did that take care of me?

"Julie claims Pearl murdered Arjuna," I said. "Julie says she's still afraid that Pearl intends to get rid of her." Barney looked at me stonily. Her face inside the coif was square and hard. "Then help her," she said.

I blew off steam by going out to look for Pat. My problem was multi- fold. For one thing, I was hooked on the case, so I would try to get to the bottom of it whether I was paid or not. I suspected Barney counted on that and had never intended to pay.

Another disquieting thought came to me. These days you need a license to blow your nose. There probably was a law against taking money to ask questions unless the State of Maine gave its approval—for a fee. It was suddenly clear: Barney would blackmail me if I were stupid enough to insist on getting paid.

Pat says I'm paranoid when I think this way. I say Pat has her head in the sand when it comes to Barney.

I settled myself on a boulder near where I intended to build my shed. I needed to calm down and think through what I had come to think of as 'my case.' The late afternoon sun was warm, the granite radiant. The apple tree I planned to situate my kitchen door behind had begun to flower. If a black fly hadn't bitten me I might have thought I was in Paradise.

One thing was clear. If Barney were willing to pay me—that is, offer to pay me—to investigate something, there was money in it somewhere. At first I had thought she might want some of Arjuna's walking-around money. But after seeing the results of Pearl's high-finance charity at Shangri-La, I realized there was some loose change there, too.

So, lots of bait for Barney, especially if the facts were free, courtesy of Brigid Donovan. But what about Pearl? Why had she been so genial? Laughing when she said she understood I had been hired to look into her affairs, paying for my trip to Nova Scotia to ease my way.

While I couldn't yet fathom Pearl's motives, I didn't doubt that I would uncover them sooner or later. Perhaps they were no more complicated than a desire to humor Julie. If Pearl were completely innocent, it's something she might do, help me to investigate her. Just to get it over with.

But who, I thought, is completely innocent?

That evening Pat and I sat by the fire sipping warm milk and honey. I had been rambling about my dilemma, wanting money and not knowing whom to stick. She said, brusquely I thought, "Just tell Pearl you changed your mind and you want the mileage she's getting from the foundation."

"But…" I said.

"Brigid," she interrupted, "suit yourself. I'm tired and I'm going to bed."

Hardly a companionable interchange.

I left before anyone was up in the morning. Left with Pearl's five new Andrew Jacksons in my pocket, them and my well used credit cards. The van was luxurious, tape deck, radio, air conditioning. All I used was the radio. Outside Pembroke the news came on. Arjuna's death was being ruled 'probable homicide.' He had been tied to the bed he lay in, the fire started with gasoline. There were no suspects yet. I wondered what had been in the bromide Pearl gave him.

The drive to the convent of St. Therese, on the outskirts of Halifax, took ten hours. I stopped at the Irving station in Amherst to fill up. Gas for the van and a cheeseburger for me.

Two images haunted me on that long and solitary drive. They were both of Julie. One concerned suttee, the violent conflagration Julie had seemed to flirt with as she trod the smoldering ruins in her diaphanous apparel. The other, also tragic, conjured, too, from the delicate clouds enveloping her, must have sprung from a movie I once saw about Isadora Duncan. I saw Julie, again and again, strangled in her own clothing as it wrapped itself in the spokes of Arthur's bike.

I wondered, idly, why Julie aroused this sense of doom in me. And, idly again, I was interested to find that my mind linked her not only with Arjuna, but also with Arthur. Or Jesus.

Maybe the link was religious. Or pseudo-religious. Julie had, apparently, played a supporting role in each man's personal Passion Play. And yet, I sensed, the roles had been very different, as different as the two men. I had only seen a photo of Arjuna, and caught but a glimpse of Arthur/Jesus. But I didn't think I was mistaken about the brazen twinkle in Arjuna's eye. Whatever else his religiosity might have meant to him, Arjuna had had fun. Not so Arthur. Arthur had been deadly serious—that word again—when he spoke of his father and meant God.

Somewhere outside Moncton, I began to reflect on all the Religious involved in this affair, from Pat and Barney at the

Cloisters, to Pearl MacDonald at Shangri-La, her granddaughter Julie, Arjuna, and Arthur. Only two, I thought wryly, were, in my book, entirely serious, and one of them, Arthur, was schizophrenic and couldn't help it. I considered, regretfully, Sister Pat's calling to be genuine. And Arthur really did believe he was Jesus. Probably from looking in the mirror. He resembled Jesus on the Holy Cards they used to give us for learning our catechism. A big Swede, silky golden hair, long lashes, ice blue eyes. Beautiful. But crazy. And dangerous, probably. Julie seemed to think so, when he called her Jezebel.

I could imagine that those almond eyes of Arjuna had sparkled with laughter as he and Julie developed her stigmata. But the only spark I could imagine kindled in Arthur's eyes might burn Julie in the very conflagration she had claimed to want. I hoped she was wise enough not to fool around with him, but feared she was too crazy to realize her vulnerability. Schizophrenic enough, maybe, to believe she was immortal. Or perhaps, just too self-centered to care.

The drive-way into St. Therese was a good two tenths of a mile long and must have cost them a bundle to keep plowed in winter. I followed the signs for 'deliveries', past formal flower beds being planted with annuals, set here and there on putting-green lawns. You could tell by the size of the oaks, that St. Therese had been around for a while. And you could tell that it enjoyed substantial support from somewhere, organized crime maybe. The only places I'd ever seen with grounds like it were the municipal gardens of Toronto and a few very ritzy resorts.

I was told by Sister Marie, the nun who took charge of the van, that Sister Agnes, Mother Superior, would see me after supper. Marie took me up to my room, a good-sized cubicle with bed, easy chair, desk, basin, chest of drawers, and closet. She told me the library would be open until ten o'clock, and that tonight I could use the Fathers' swimming pool, if I had thought to bring my swimsuit. I hadn't. The monastery, she said, was across the road.

I had an hour until dinner, so I washed up and went to the library. I had forgotten how sweet the vow of poverty could be, and was amused to find myself envious of the luxury and ease of my surroundings.

Pearl MacDonald had been born in New Glasgow. I wanted to get a feel for her background. I discovered that the New Glasgow paper, *The Evening News*, was on micro fiche. I decided to return to the library after supper to look at some old issues.

The Mother Superior of St. Therese was large and stern, but cordial. She said Pearl MacDonald had called her that morning and asked that she, Sister Agnes, talk to me about the circumstances of Pearl's upbringing at the convent. She had, Sister Agnes said, looked into the records in order to do this. She herself had never had the pleasure of making Pearl MacDonald's acquaintance.

Pearl, said Sister Agnes, had been orphaned when she was nine years old. She was not from one of the better New Glasgow families, but the parish priest, recognizing what a bright little girl she was, had brought her to St. Therese. She had lived there, without incident, until at age seventeen, she had enrolled as a student at St. Francis Xavier in Antigonish.

I waited for the rest. We were sitting in the Mother Superior office, a room as imposing as Pearl MacDonald's at Shangri-La. More imposing: the ceilings were higher. But Sister Agnes continued to sit silent, stolid and silent, her hands hidden in the sleeves of her habit.

"What," I ventured after a while, "about the baby?"

Sister Agnes removed a tissue from the recesses of her sleeve and hawked into it. "You seem to know about that already." She held up her hand to stop my response. "I called Sister MacDonald back. She affirmed she has already told you about the infant."

"You brought him up too?" I asked.

"Yes."

"But he didn't go to St. Francis Xavier."

"No. He was a very bright youngster, and one of our benefactors," she nodded her recognition of the opulence around us, "offered to underwrite his education. He went to Dalhousie."

"Who was this benefactor?"

She was prepared for the question. "One of the best Halifax

families, the Comptons."

I wondered where the Holy Family would rate on Sister Agnes' scale of better and best. No account, probably.

Pearl MacDonald had been born on the Fourth of July. No big deal in New Glasgow, Nova Scotia, Canada. I found the birth announcement in the *New Glasgow Evening News*. "Angus and Pearl MacDonald. Baby Girl." About eight MacDonald babies had been born that week and three had daddies named Angus. The year was 1929.

I discovered the shocking story about fifteen minutes—or nine years— later. The headline wavered into focus on the lighted screen "Man Killed in Blaze. Angus MacDonald Arson Victim."

It happened in the spring of 1938. Investigators discovered that the fire had been started with gasoline. Angus MacDonald had, apparently, been tied to the bed where his charred body was found.

In the end his widow had been tried for his murder and found guilty. The jury must have pitied her. She served a light sentence of only five years. Angus had been a violent and drunken man who beat her and their three little girls, Faith, Hope and Charity. No Pearl. Wrong MacDonald.

I went to sleep that night troubled by the similarity of circumstance between the deaths of Arjuna and Angus MacDonald. In my dreams I rang the changes of the personalities involved, Pearl MacDonald of Shangri-La my leading note: As Faith, as Hope, as Charity, and as the poor convicted mother. The mother's name eluded me in my dreams. Not until I woke at four, tangled in my covers, sweating, did I remember: The mother's name was Pearl.

At breakfast, Sister Marie said to me, "Mother wishes to see you."

'Mother' told me my van was loaded. She asked did I know how to get to Eskasoni, the Indian reservation on Cape Breton Island.

I said I had a map, what I didn't have was money.

"Oh, dear," replied Sister Agnes, "Sister MacDonald said she had given you a hundred dollars. American."

"Yeah, like I said. To drive up to Cape Breton and back, I'll need more money."

From the same dark recess where she kept her tissues, Mother Superior drew forth an envelope marked "Emergency." She extracted some pretty Canadian bills. "Will fifty cover your expenses?" she asked.

"Maybe," I said. "But I'd rather play it safe. Give me a hundred. What I don't need, I can always return. You can buy a flat of pansies with it."

Chapter 5

I turned off Route 104 at New Glasgow. Taking a long chance, I asked at the Irving station where I would go to pay my property tax. "Pictou," he said.

The clerk in the tax office was helpful. No problem, she said. If they owned property, my Nova Scotia cousins Faith and Hope, nee MacDonald, would be easy to locate. Their farm, she told me after a little dusty research, was near Scotsburn. Born MacDonald, Faith and Hope had remained MacDonald, the clerk informed me, and together they ran a small sheep farm. She showed me, on my map, how to get there.

Their road, dirt for the last few miles, was pocked with holes and waled like corduroy. Fields on either side, lush with new grass, looked like the first day of creation. I knew I had reached the MacDonald farm when on my left I saw a flock of sheep with a dozen or so new lambs bouncing about worrying their dams.

I had imagined white clapboard and rockers on a wide front porch, so I almost missed the house, a berm house, the slope of earth reaching to the window ledges so unkempt it looked as if the house might be sinking. Dilapidated, but dandelions in the shaggy grass seemed to smile a welcome.

The barn was larger than the house, larger and even more ramshackle. I hesitated before entering the gloomy womb-like space. Once inside, I had to stop to let my eyes grow used to the dimness. The sounds I heard were comforting: bleating, the rustle of hay, women's soft voices murmuring encouragement.

The activity was in a birthing stall at the back. Two elderly women knelt beside a sheep in labor. I realized one of the women had her arm inside the creature. Both women crooned soothing platitudes. Soon I saw a hoof appear, then a larger mass, black and wet, the head. When it was out, the lamb stood, shakily, on spindly legs, and the mother began to wash it. A moment later the placenta emerged and the woman who had assisted the birth scooped it up in a shovel. "Well done, Violet," she murmured. Then, as she turned to leave, she saw me. "Good Lord!" she exclaimed, spilling the still warm placenta on my pants and shoes.

They insisted on washing me clean. I felt like the new born lamb pummeled by its mother's tongue. Only I had two mothers worrying over me. I did, finally, manage to get my way, at least to the extent of changing my clothes in private. When I emerged, Faith put my bloody garments in the washer, and Hope poured me a cup of tea.

They could have been Pearl MacDonald's sisters, they were of the same Celtic stock, fine boned, finely textured skin, and fine-spun hair that might once have been red but now was silver. They claimed never to have heard of a Pearl MacDonald. "We are so sorry we can't help you," they assured me. "We have no American cousins," they said.

The room where we sat with our tea was a large workroom. Partly for dairy: Stainless steel kettles hung from hooks near a large stainless steel sink. And partly for wool: Plastic grain bags of wool, carded and uncarded, spilled their contents in one corner where a spinning wheel and stool faced a small television set. By the round oak table where we drank our tea, a loom held what might have been a blanket or a rug. Hanging clusters of herbs scented the air.

I explained diffidently, feeling reluctant to challenge them, about Pearl MacDonald of Surry, Maine, and how I was running all these errands for her in Nova Scotia, bringing what the rich in the States had discarded so that the poor in Nova Scotia could live.

They nodded and clucked sympathetically and asked whether

I wouldn't like a scone with my tea.

"Her granddaughter, Julie, wanted to come with me," I improvised. "She wanted to see where her grandmother grew up. In Pictou, I heard about your place here, and I thought, MacDonald, maybe there's a connection."

Faith and Hope smiled knowingly at one another. Faith explained. "MacDonald, Mrs. Donovan, in these parts that's like Smith."

I pretended embarrassed confusion. Hope asked, "How old is your Julie. Is she just a child?"

Faith looked at her severely. Hope said, "I asked because I thought we could send her some mittens. Mrs. Donovan could tell her she found two old ladies who could have been her aunties."

I explained Julie to them, leaving out bizarre details like stigmata. I said she was lovely and about twenty-two. I didn't mention she was mad as a hatter. Faith and Hope nodded fondly at one another. They liked hearing about Julie.

"She and her grandmother, this Pearl MacDonald, they don't get along too well," I said. "I think Julie wanted to, well, I guess get closer to her roots."

That made them beam.

I decided to take a risk. "Last night at the convent of St. Therese I was looking through back issues of the *New Glasgow Evening News* and I came across this terrible tragedy. A man, Angus MacDonald, he was burned to death. There were three little girls, Faith, Hope, and Charity. But the mother's name was Pearl. When I heard a Faith and Hope MacDonald ran this sheep farm, well I thought I had the right family."

My little speech wiped the smiles from their faces. Faith responded. She said, crisply, "You're a snoop!"

I had let myself be deceived by their wrinkles and gentle demeanor. These two old ladies with the grit to make a go of a small sheep farm were about as gentle as the arsenic in *Arsenic and Old Lace*. I played my Julie card again.

"For Julie, yes," I admitted. "She came to me. She said she was afraid of her grandmother, Pearl MacDonald. She asked me to discover what I could about her background. She said she was afraid Pearl intended to murder her."

Consternation.

The spokeswoman, Faith, asked, "Murder? Why murder?"

I explained a little of the tangled web of emotion and ambition in Surry. I realized as I spoke that a little was all I knew. "Julie had taken up with a guru, a man named Arjuna."

The two exchanged another of their knowing looks. But they said nothing.

"Julie felt that Pearl was jealous."

"You don't mean to imply," said Faith, "a, um, sexual entanglement between this Arjuna and Julie?"

Old lace led me to lie, "Oh no!" I said. "Envy. Envy and fear. Julie felt Pearl was anxious about the continued success of her own charitable works. Arjuna, I guess, was very popular and had planned to build a temple in the next town, Soperton."

They nodded, knowingly, again.

"Julie's an awfully sweet kid," I said. Faith and Hope, doting, smiled. "Still, I thought she was a little crazy, thinking her own grandmother would do her harm, let alone murder her. But then, right before I left to come up here, Arjuna died. In a fire. Arson. He had been tied to the bed."

Hope swayed in her chair. She reached out to Faith for support.

"Frankly," I said, "I went out of my way to find you. After I read that story. I thought you could help. If," I added, looking hopefully from one to the other, "you would."

Faith took charge again. She squeezed the hand Hope had laid on hers. "I don't know what help we can give. If Julie's afraid she can always come home."

"Home?" I echoed.

Julie had spent summers in Scotsburn since she was a little girl. Faith and Hope took me upstairs to show me her bedroom. It belonged to an adolescent girl, the posters on the wall beginning to yellow with age. A dressing table, skirted in organdy and ruffles, so out of keeping with the rest of the house, held an array of perfume bottles and tools to color nails, cheeks, eyes and hair.

Back at the oak table they paged through albums of old photos and I learned the history of Julie's exploits as she passed from infancy through adolescence.

I had hoped the sisters might indicate something about Julie's mental health. But they seemed to regard her as the measure of perfection. I said, "Julie strikes me as a little out of touch with reality."

They assured me this was not so. I debated telling them about the stigmata. "Did she ever express a desire to join a convent? When she was a girl."

They exchanged a pleased and knowing look. "I think Julie may have been having you on, Mrs. Donovan," they said.

"She's a tease," said Hope.

"She never means harm," Faith assured me. "It's just her way."

"Not everyone understands such high spirits."

How many families had nurtured sociopaths by doting blindly I wondered. Perhaps as many as had nurtured them through bizarre strictness. Or perhaps they are born not made. Maybe, as Julie kept insisting, I just didn't get it. Her aunties got it: Julie could do no wrong.

"She hasn't visited for a while?" I ventured.

They shook their heads sadly. I waited. Hope broke the silence. "That Pearl," she said bitterly.

"Tch, tch," Faith admonished.

"Well," said Hope defensively, "it's true." She turned and looked me in the eye, perhaps for support, to be an ally against Faith's Goody-Two-Shoes. "Pearl invited her down to that Xanadu place she has there in the States."

"Hope, don't!" warned Faith.

"Shangri-La," I corrected.

"Shangri-La! Xanadu! It's corrupt!" Hope rushed on, ignoring her sister. "I have, after all seen pictures of the place."

For a while I let them quarrel undisturbed about the nature of good works. They seemed to hold the same opinion: Anything beyond what the necessities of life required, one gave to charity, and didn't talk about it. Where they differed was on how closely you scrutinized your neighbor. Hope judged Pearl harshly. Faith judged Hope: "That Shangri-La place is between Charity and God, Hope, and none of your business!"

Arguing, they had referred to Pearl as Charity. I asked them about it.

They turned, flushed, to face me. Faith, abashed as she remembered my presence; Hope, indignant. Hope said, "Yes! Charity. She took our mother's name after the, uh, accident."

They had gone too far to pretend any longer, and Faith murmured something about the cock crowing three times, before she began to tell the tale.

Faith was the oldest of three girls born a year apart to an impoverished family of fisher folk in Pictou. The father—Hope told this part—was a drunk and violent to boot. He beat the mother mercilessly in front of the children, and, often enough, he beat the girls too. One Christmas Eve, right before the war, Angus MacDonald had come home drunk. He began by smashing the Christmas tree, a little thing the girls had cut in the woods behind the house and decorated with nuts, pine cones and shells they had collected. Faith was twelve and had for years tried to protect everyone, her mother, her smaller sisters, their good name in the community. When Angus, after stamping on the tree, picked it up and began to wield it like a club, beating the mother on her head and shoulders with it, Charity jumped to the mother's defense pummeling the father, flailing his thigh and buttocks with her fists. Faith caught her and tried to pull her away.

Hope had become quite agitated in the telling of the scene. "Charity fought back. She said she'd rather die than see her mother beaten again. Father, he turned on Charity, he picked her up and just tossed her, he tossed her through the window."

Hope began to cry. Faith pulled her close. "We were able to get out of the cottage then," she said.

Hope interrupted, "Faith pushed mother and me out the back door. We went to grandmother's house. Faith stayed to help Charity."

Charity was bleeding, but no bones were broken and the two girls had proceeded to their grandmother's where they had sought refuge before in similar circumstances.

The village had been awakened early Christmas day by the fire. When the evidence of arson was discovered along with the fact that Angus had been tied to the bed he had fallen on in a drunken stupor, the mother had been indicted for murder.

"She didn't do it," the sisters assured me.

Then who did, I asked.

No one, they said.

I asked how it could have been an accident.

It was clear they had long ago worked out an answer that satisfied them. Angus, in a drunken rage, had himself set fire to the house.

"But, he was tied to the bed," I said.

Hope replied, "He did that after."

"You mean, your father committed suicide?"

"Mrs. Donovan," said Faith with quiet authority, "what we believe happened is that Father started to burn down the house, but, drunk as he was, poor man, he became confused. We believe he hallucinated, perhaps imagining he was at sea, in a storm most likely, and that he tied himself to the bed thinking he was tying himself to his boat. He couldn't swim," she added.

The explanation might have been comforting to the grieving family, but to me it seemed far-fetched. I said, "Your mother pleaded guilty."

The sisters erupted in speech together. Faith, in time, took over. Their mother had pleaded guilty to protect Charity. People were saying that the little girl had set the fire and tied her father to the bed.

"But you told me she was only nine."

"Of course, Mrs. Donovan, the whole thing was absurd," Faith assured me. "She was so young, and besides, she had been hurt in the fight."

"Why would people even think such a thing?" I asked.

Hope answered. "She told everyone she'd done it. That's why."

"So your mother sacrificed herself for Charity, even though Charity could not possibly have been responsible?"

"Mrs. Donovan," Faith said again, but even more emphatically, "the whole thing was absurd."

The grandmother had kept the two older girls when their mother went to prison. The local priest had arranged for Charity to be taken to the orphanage of St. Therese in Halifax. I gathered that her sisters believed this had been done to protect Charity rather than because she had been so exceptionally bright.

"So many people continued to blame her," said Hope.

"Everyone knew, of course, that our mother would never have done such a thing," added Faith.

"They would have believed that he had done it himself, which of course he had done, but Mother was afraid to risk Charity."

"And didn't want to expose Charity to the trial."

"So she took the blame and went to prison."

"Although only for five years, the jury was very sympathetic."

"And Charity had her start in life," Hope ended tartly.

Before I left, they fed me goat's milk cheese with herbs, bread baked that morning, and milk. It reminded me of the Cloisters and Pat. They gave me an address where I could find their mother. Smelt Brook, Cape Breton.

"She must be getting old," I said.

"But sharp as a tack," Hope assured me. They gave me several skeins of yarn to bring her and a gossamer shawl Faith had knitted.

Chapter 6

The drive up from New Glasgow was long and hard, Route 104 being mostly two lanes and heavily trafficked. I amused myself by eating the cheese and bread that Faith and Hope had insisted on giving me. That and mulling over what they had told me.

That Angus MacDonald more than fifty years ago had died the same way Arjuna had just died—in a fire, tied to his bed—mystified me. I wondered wryly whether Arjuna, too, had not known how to swim. I could understand how the sisters Faith and Hope could assuage their pain by such an absurd reconstruction of their father's death. But that it could be a coincidence, both men dying the same way, was as inconceivable to me as someone committing such a bizarre crime twice.

Candidates for the role of double murderer were also difficult to imagine. Mrs. MacDonald, wife of Angus MacDonald, would be nearly ninety, and was surely out of the running. It was perhaps possible that Pearl as a child had done what she apparently claimed to have done, eliminate a brutal tyrant who happened to be her father. But surely, if Pearl *had* killed Arjuna, she would have thought of another.and less conspicuous way to do it. She wasn't stupid. Besides, it was Pearl who suggested I come to Nova Scotia. Not that she would have imagined I might uncover her past, I thought. Later, when it was too late, I realized I hadn't given people enough credit for craftiness. Mother Superior knew nothing beyond the Halifax Social Register. I just assumed Pearl must believe that would satisfy me. Pride, the deadliest of the deadly sins.

The only person left was Julie of the many veils and stigmata. Her aunties claimed she was unaware of the tragedy in her family's past, that they had moved from Pictou to Scotsburn in order to protect her. But it seemed improbable to me that Julie was entirely ignorant of that tragic event. Careful as they might have tried to be, it was too heavy a burden to carry without stumbling. Faith and Hope had, without doubt, let slip some hint that would make a bright child curious. Curious enough, perhaps, to look for answers, and to find some.

But what, I thought, if that were so? Julie's knowing about her great-grandfather's murder would hardly make her a murderer. In fact, Julie's knowledge might have been at the bottom of her fear of Pearl. On the other hand, I mused, she might have used her knowledge to frame Pearl for Arjuna's murder.

On that reasoning, it might also be that Pearl, intelligent as she was, could imagine that, by imitating an earlier crime, she would create a good defense: Who would ever believe she could be so stupid? Not me.

Then I started all over again, down the list of suspects, weighing the possibilities, discounting the absurdities, coming up with zip. All the way to the Canso Causeway. Then the beauty of Cape Breton took over and gave my brain a rest.

I reached Eskasoni a little before six that evening. Drugged on the glories of Cape Breton, high on the experience of two ferry rides, across the Little and the Grand Narrows, I was unprepared for the long dusty road that was the reservation. I stopped at the first store and asked directions to the church.

Straight through town, past the ball field, up the hill on my left, the young man behind the counter told me. He added shyly that Father's housekeeper, Yolande, was his cousin.

The Indian woman who answered my knock at the back door of the white clapboard parish house admitted to being Yolande and cousin to the young man at the store. She laughed when she talked and said I was lucky to have caught her, she was about to leave for home. But she insisted that I stay for supper, she would fix it for me. Father, however, was away, and so I should visit the church while she prepared my meal.

My protests being useless, I made my way across the parking lot to the church. I was glad that I had. The iconography was Native American. Jesus and Mary as Indians I liked better than as sixteenth century aristocratic Italians, the Medici or the Borgia. Another woman, professorial in sensible shoes, skirt and cardigan, was busy photographing the Stations of the Cross.

From the back she seemed to be my age, her hair, streaked with gray, pulled severely into a bun. When she turned, though, I saw my mistake. She was young, mid-thirties maybe. Horn-rimmed glasses secured by a gold chain, like her bun, suggested maturity. But black as the glasses were, they couldn't hide the youthful glint of her almond eyes. For some reason she reminded me of Julie. The eyes, maybe, the shape of them. Or her mouth, not as ripe as Julie's, but finely molded like hers. Julie when I met her made me think of a child playing dress-up. This woman, too, seemed to be acting the part of someone older. I wondered why.

"Aren't they marvelous?" the woman said. Her eyes met mine and held them. They were blue. Blue as Sister Pat's. But her hair was black, jet black and silver, and very curly. Here and there a strand had sprung free from the knot, wiry as an airedale's, but prettier, and soft.

As I stared she laughed and pulled a card from the pocket of her cardigan. "Suzanne Compton," she said, handing the card to me.

I pried my eyes loose from hers and studied the card, all three lines. It said, 'Suzanne Compton, PhD., Anthropology, Dalhousie University, Halifax.' There was a phone number.

She said many of her students were Micmacs. "I'm interested," she confided, "in the religious adaptations indigenous people make to imported religions." Like me, she heartily approved of the Micmac iconographic 'adaptations.' I said if I ever got back to Halifax I'd be sure to look her up.

Returning to the house, I discovered Yolande's cousin and another young man emptying the van of the appliances I had brought. My supper was ready, cold sliced chicken, salad and fruit. Yolande sat and drank tea while I ate. She thought I should stay the night, but I still had a couple hours of daylight left, and I wanted to push on toward Smelt Brook and my interview with Mrs. MacDonald.

I got as far as Baddeck. There, hardly able to stay awake, I stopped at a bed and breakfast, at the end of Shore Road, right on the water. Another Mrs. MacDonald, a widow. She had an empty room. She rented them in summer, she said, for company. She didn't get much of mine. I went upstairs and passed out.

Going around the Cabot Trail counter clock-wise is scary if you're afraid of heights, and I am. For much of the trip I felt as if I might at any moment plunge a thousand feet to a watery death. I stopped frequently at scenic turn-outs to collect myself, and to enjoy the amazing vistas: rugged mountains and valleys robed in the rich greens of a climax forest; and infinity, dimly seen in the crack between ocean and sky where they met, one immensity of blue joining another. I looked for bald eagles, as I always do. But all I saw, gliding in the distance, were gulls.

At Neil Harbour I stopped at the office of the Victoria Co-op Fisheries to ask directions. "Mrs. Pearl MacDonald, now she would be that widow from away who lives by herself?" the girl at the window asked. I said I didn't know, but my Mrs. MacDonald must be getting on to ninety.

"Oh, she's the one, then," the young woman assured me.

Pearl MacDonald lived on a dirt road overlooking the sea, the house small, two rooms, shingled with cedar that was wrinkled and warped and weathered to a fine silver color. I knocked and halooed a while before I caught her attention. I could see her through the gauzy window curtains. She stood at the counter kneading dough. Like the shingles, her body was warped and wrinkled, her hair silvery. She kneaded with gusto, but was apparently hard of hearing. I stopped being polite and rapped the window with my knuckles.

She was delighted with the wool I had brought. She gestured to shelves piled with knitted garments "Sell them at Lauraine's," she said. "Craft store, outside Neil's Harbour."

We had tea sitting at a window overlooking the ocean. The

bread was a crusty sourdough, the butter sweet. I decided to retire to Smelt Brook myself one day. Maybe I could board with Mrs. MacDonald. She seemed pleased to give me tea. And surprisingly incurious about the reason for my visit.

"This morning," she said softly, "there were whales." She nodded off toward Spain. "Too bad you missed that."

"Yesterday," I ventured, "when I visited Faith and Hope, they told me about, about the tragedy."

"It isn't often, this time of year, you see whales."

"Oh. No, I expect not. Mrs. MacDonald, I came to Nova Scotia for your daughter. Uh, Charity, but she calls herself…"

"Pearl. Yes I know. Let me warm our tea."

She puttered at the stove a while in silence. I reflected that the aunties had started to open up when I mentioned Julie. I decided to give it a try. "It was really your great granddaughter Julie who suggested I come and visit," I said, stretching the truth.

"Julie should be more careful of the companions she chooses," said Mrs. MacDonald. "Do have some more bread and butter."

"Arjuna died," I said, surprised that she knew about Arjuna, the only shady character I could think of connected with Julie. Wondering who would have told her about him and how much they would have told. I doubted this crusty Scotswoman would have much truck with Buddhism and even less with stigmata.

"Is that his name?" Mrs. MacDonald said, wiping clean the knife she had used to slice the bread. "He is very odd."

"He died in much the same way as your husband," I said, risking silencing her in the hope that she might instead begin to talk.

"I never thought it was wise, Julie going to the States."

It was unclear to me how much the oddness of our repartee had to do with Mrs. MacDonald's hearing and how much with her reluctance to impart information. I tried again, "Have you ever been to Shangri-La?"

Mrs. MacDonald grunted. "Shangri-La," she repeated disgustedly.

"Well, it's not really. I mean, they call it Shangri-La because it, well, it used to be such a mess out there."

"It's corrupt!" exclaimed Mrs. MacDonald, echoing her

daughter Hope.

I wondered why these women spoke so certainly of corruption regarding Pearl's endeavors. I didn't like what Pearl did, milking foundations in the name of 'the poor.' And I certainly didn't like the crystal doorknobs and swimming pool for visiting philanthropists. But when I think corrupt, I think bribes and drugs and prostitution. Since the New England states went into the numbers racket on a big scale, aka Tri-State Lottery, even that no longer seemed corrupt to me.

Mrs. MacDonald returned with the teapot, in a cozy, and more bread and butter. We rocked silently for a while. The clean austerity of her cottage, of her life, pleased me. Like a mild astringent for the soul, it was refreshing. It came to me in the silence why Hope and Mrs. MacDonald thought Shangri-La was corrupt. It was the same reason Luther thought Rome was corrupt, why Calvin and all the Presbyterians after him had thought so too. The Scots heritage was strong in Nova Scotia and the bitterness against the folderol of Anglicanism and Catholicism. Genuflection probably would rile a stiff-backed woman like Pearl MacDonald, never mind painted statues, swimming pools and crystal doorknobs. It must have galled them, Pearl's association with the Church. It maybe broke their hearts when Julie went south, too, so to speak.

Mrs. MacDonald began to talk. "She went to University, you know, down to St. F.X."

It took me a moment to register that she was telling me about Pearl and to discover that, whatever her religious discomforts, she was proud of this recusant daughter of hers.

Mrs. MacDonald plucked the cozy off the pot and poured us more tea. "It's in Antigonish. You pass it on your way home. Stop by and see. They remember her. Remember me too. Send a card at Christmas. My birthday too." She rose and went into the back room. A moment later she emerged with a large cardboard box.

"Let me help you with that."

But she had already deposited the box on the table between us. It held the Christmas cards and the birthday cards, dozens of them, and several photo albums. For the next hour I looked at pictures of Pearl MacDonald. Many were of Pearl as a girl at the convent-orphanage of St. Therese. These were all black and white and had been much handled. They were, I suddenly realized, photos that had lived, with their owner, in prison. For the first time it came home to me just how appalling Mrs. MacDonald's situation had been.

In full color I saw Pearl as a young woman in India. Mrs. MacDonald lingered with special pride on these. "She wore a sari," Mrs. MacDonald said, pointing at one. "Once she could speak Hindi. Felt it gave her a right. Some wore saris as couldn't speak a word of the language." That, her tone said, was presumptuous and therefore wrong. In a couple of these Indian photos, Pearl was with a young man who resembled Arjuna. I asked to look more closely at one.

"His name was Arjuna, too," Mrs. MacDonald said.

"Yeah, that's what I thought."

There were many photos of Shangri-La documenting its transformation from Tobacco Road to Ford Foundation. These Mrs. MacDonald kept pushing toward the bottom. "You don't care much for Pearl's work at H.O.P.E.," I said.

She grunted. "H.O.P.E.'s okay. I get the paper. Read your history, too," she said slyly. "It's this nonsense!" She stabbed her finger at the Greek tympanum over Shangri-La's front door. "Swimming pools! Pride," she added darkly.

We chatted for another hour, rocking gently together, lulled by the beat of waves on the cobblestone beach across the way. Mrs. MacDonald holding one conversation, me another. Most of the time. After a while I let go, felt myself drift into the comfort of this crone's home, so spare, so tidy, so easily strong and durable.

As I let myself drift, I let go, too, of my reason for coming to Smelt Brook. I lost all sense of Mrs. MacDonald as a person with a history. She had, in my mind, transcended her own life. The woman who had served a five-year prison term for murdering her husband lived on micro-fiche, not in this weathered cabin, not in this weathered body rocking next to mine.

Our conversation flowed gently as a brook, my contribution an idle question falling, like a leaf, on the moving surface now and then. Mrs. MacDonald liked to talk about her daughter. She called her Charity. She said she objected when Charity began to call herself Pearl. But a small pleased smile bent her lips. Perhaps she found in Pearl's successful life some compensation for the sacrifice she had made, a vicarious fulfillment. Whether or not young Pearl had killed the brutal Angus MacDonald, her mother's meek acceptance of blame had spared the child. Not just spared her, had provided the opportunity of a fuller life, broader horizons. An opportunity sister Hope still resented.

Around four, I finally managed to take my leave. Mrs. MacDonald again enjoined me to stop in Antigonish to visit the Coady Institute. "It's right there, where you get off the highway. St. F.X. Anyone can tell you. They know all about my daughter there."

By the time I regained the Cabot Trail, I had begun to fret. Something kept nagging at me. Something important. I kept coming back to the fact that all along Mrs. MacDonald had known who I was, that she'd read my history of H.O.P.E. Who, I wondered had told her to expect me. Pearl? But how would Pearl have known I was going there? That left the sisters, Faith and Hope. But they didn't know me as someone who had written a history of the community where Pearl worked.

It occurred to me, finally, that my puzzlement sprang from 'ageism.' I wouldn't accept that someone ninety could put that information together unaided. I chided myself. But then I discovered it wasn't my 'ageism' that had caused my uneasiness. In fact, acknowledging just how quick Mrs. MacDonald was made me feel even more uneasy. Something about that interview wasn't right, but I couldn't figure out what. Maybe later, maybe later it would come.

I coasted into Inverness a little after five. The day was still warm enough for a walk along the beach. I decided to find a motel and stay the night right there. Lucky for me I did. I ran into Professor Compton again. Anthropologist, Dalhousie University Professor Compton. Professor Compton who maybe wanted to look as if she were old enough and dry enough to be tenure material. I decided, seeing her again, I could adjust to teaching somewhere—anywhere—they wanted to keep Suzanne Compton on for life.

Chapter 7

I ran into Professor Compton on the beach at Inverness. I didn't recognize her. Her hair had been liberated. Maybe it had liberated itself. It stood out from her head—in serried ranks I thought, the waves so tight and still so wild. Like an Egyptian Queen, I thought. Exotic anyway. She wore indigo trousers of some silky material and a heavy woven jacket of Guatemalan cloth, jeweled colors, emerald green, ruby red, sapphire.

"Hallo!" she called as I passed to the ocean side of her, barely nodding a greeting. "You don't recognize me!"

She had stopped. I turned to face her. It was the eyes I recognized, the familiar way they held mine captive.

"Suzanne Compton," she said. "We met yesterday, in Eskasoni, at the church."

"Yeah. Hi," I said. I reclaimed my eyes, with difficulty, and inspected my shoes. Tennis shoes and, just as I feared, barely three weeks old and a hole had begun to form at my little toe. Her naked toes, quite close to mine, were long and prehensile. Her trousers were rolled, her ankles exposed. Slender as wrists, they didn't seem at all like good tenure material.

"You staying in Inverness?" she asked.

"Yeah," I chatted.

"Oh good. Let's have supper together."

We walked a while on the beach first. Suzanne did most of the talking. Her voice was soft and slightly furry, but her diction was clear and Canadian. She was writing a paper, she said, on the adaptability correlate of major religions in the context of traditional cultures and/or indigenous populations. I said, oh yeah? Politely. "Your research bring you to Inverness?" I asked.

In Inverness, the 'major religion' under Suzanne's scrutiny was Buddhism. The 'traditional culture' adapting it was the half Americanized Scots-Irish population.

"Buddhism," I said skeptically. "Here?"

"After we eat," Suzanne promised, "I'll show you."

We cobbled a supper together at the market: cheese and biscuits, Granny Smiths, pickles, juice and two Cadburys for dessert. We had chosen the same motel on the edge of town, and we stopped there, me for a jacket, Suzanne for shoes. She said we could walk to our picnic site and to the object of her research in Inverness, a Buddhist temple in progress.

A half mile out of town, she struck off toward the sea on a rutted track through a hay field. It ended at a bluff, thirty feet or so above the surf. We walked another half mile along the edge of the palisade to where a piece of granite, dropped by an ancient glacier, provided table and seating for our meal. A doe and her fawn, curious but not alarmed at our presence, continued to browse nearby.

Our conversation over biscuits and cheese was mostly literary. Suzanne professed a great admiration for Françoise Sagan, especially her novel *Aimez Vous Brahms?*, which, it so happened, she was just then reading.

"Are you familiar with the story?" she asked, pulling from the pocket of her jacket a paperback copy of it, in French.

"Well," I said, "I saw the movie." A silly love affair between a young man and a much older woman.

"Don't tell me how it ends, " said Suzanne.

"You mean," I said gloomily, "you don't know?"

"Oh, God! " Suzanne exclaimed, and she leaned against me for a moment. I could feel the softness of her breast against my arm. "Hets are so conflicted!"

"Say what?" I cried.

"Hets," she murmured, those ripe lips so close to my ear I

could feel her breath as she uttered the word.

"Oh, yeah," I said. "Hets."

She meant like in 'them,' 'those guys,' 'the others.'

My mouth felt suddenly dry. The heat in my groin must have dried it. Dried my brain, too. I turned. Her lips, full and slightly parted, met mine.

"Yeah," I said again—later. When I was able.

I didn't trust Francoise Sagan. Sagan's my age, exactly. She wrote that silly fable when she was in her forties. Besides, it was Ingrid Bergman playing the older woman. Ingrid Bergman never wore tennis shoes in her life, and if she ever did, I guarantee there weren't any holes in them.

Suzanne put her hand on my cheek. "Hello there," she said. "You want to see the temple?"

We came on it from the back. There wasn't much to see, it was just another building site, rubble and material everywhere. I said I was surprised that Buddhism had made in-roads into Nova Scotia. Suzanne pointed out that temples had sprung up in many unlikely places. Vermont for one, she said.

"That's true," I replied. "They're building a temple where I live in Maine. It's just a hamlet. Soperton."

"Oh, I know about that," she said. "Have you lived in Soperton long?"

"Uh, actually I don't live there yet," I admitted. I told her about the Soperton planning board and their reluctance to approve plans to build condominiums around the temple. She seemed interested. "The old timers didn't seem to think much of the Buddhist monk who was leading the effort," I remarked. "Arjuna was his name."

After a long pause, Suzanne said, "They never did."

"Come again?"

She had turned and started to walk back toward the cliff, her body a silhouette against the fiery disk of the setting sun. I ran to catch up with her.

"Are we going back the way we came?" I asked.

She stopped, facing the horizon and the sun, a small dome now, riding the distant waves.

"You okay?" I asked.

She turned to me, her face dissolved in shadow. Behind her, saffron, scarlet and orange suffused the sky.

"Let's go by the road," she said. "It will be dark soon."

In the dusk, at the road, I read the builder's sign. Compton Brothers, Ltd., it said. Halifax, Nova Scotia. Edward MacDonald, Architect.

Suzanne remained silent for most of the long walk home. At the grocery on the edge of town, she suggested we buy a bottle of wine. "Or beer, if you prefer," she said. She stood in a spill of light at the window, looking young and beautiful, tender and wild. Looking dangerous.

"Uh, no thanks," I said. "But you go ahead."

"Oh, you have to get something."

"Uh, milk. I'd like some milk."

She laughed merrily. Like at one of the Marx Brothers, Chico maybe. If I remembered right, he had holes in his shoes a lot, too. "Well, a Coke," I said, like moving into Big Time.

She really thought that was funny.

At the motel Suzanne said, "Your room or mine?"

"I go to bed awfully early," I said.

"Is that like, 'How do you like your eggs in the morning?'" She had linked her arm through mine. She was a couple inches taller than I, maybe five eight or nine. She leaned into my face. Her hair, tangled filaments of reflected light, made a cloud of rainbows in my eyes.

"Not," I said, "exactly." Before when she closed in on me, my mouth had gone dry; now I felt moisture puddle my palms and armpits. "More like I get up real early and read, so…"

The cloud of rainbows lifted. "Oh!" said Suzanne. A pause. "You're serious. My place then. I'll get some ice to keep the beer cold." She laughed, "And the Coke…and me.

"You in the program?" she asked after she returned. She had settled herself on one of the beds saying probably I'd be more comfortable if I were to lie there beside her, and I had said, pulling up a chair, maybe later.

"Yeah, I'm in the program," I replied, puzzled. "Are you?"

"Here's to the program!" Suzanne raised her bottle of beer and clicked it against my glass. "No. But a lot of my students are. The lucky ones are. My life," she said, "might be unmanageable, but I'm not ready to let anyone else have a whack at it. Not even a higher power."

I had gone over the scene at the building site many times on our mostly silent walk home. I had thought of a lot of questions. I began with, "You any relation to Compton Brothers?"

"Do I look like a Compton Brother?" she said playfully.

"I take it, then, that you are," I shot back—playful, too, like a porcupine. "What about Eddie MacDonald, the architect."

"What about him?"

"You know him?"

"Not in the biblical sense." She finished her beer and got another one from the ice bucket. "We're awfully cheerful tonight," she said.

"Sorry. It's past my bedtime. How well do you know Eddie MacDonald?"

"Not well. Wrong question. He's my cousin."

I couldn't compute her information. It wasn't possible that Pearl MacDonald of H.O.P.E., reared in the convent orphanage, daughter of the Mrs. MacDonald I'd had tea with just a few hours earlier—it wasn't possible that that Pearl MacDonald could be Suzanne Compton's aunt. But Pearl MacDonald, I knew, was Eddie MacDonald's mother. I remembered what Pearl had confided, on that ride to Machias. Eddie was the result of rape, and Eddie, too, had been brought up in the orphanage.

"Eddie MacDonald's *father* is your uncle?" I asked her.

"He was."

"He's dead?"

"Oh, God!" Suzanne exclaimed. "I need to get drunk. I should have bought wine."

She reached over and with the palm of her hand, she brought my head closer. "Let's make love," she said, her appeal so earnest it was child-like.

I wondered, if she hadn't run into me, who Suzanne might have corralled into her bed that night.

"Oh, poor Brigid!" She let me go. "Don't pay any attention to me," she said. Her fingers began to play patty-cake on my knee. "I mean, I really would like to. Make love with you. But I know it's not on. I'm just having a really hard time right now."

She had started to cry, discreet little tears, at first, that formed and spilled from the fine dark lashes. Then, like a storm that breaks with little warning, the torrent came. I moved onto the bed and took her in my arms. What else could I have done?

Aimez Vous Brahms?, the movie version, haunted our love making, mine anyway, not that Suzanne bore any resemblance to Tony Perkins. Just her youth, and my age. But she made love as if she meant it, and in a while I stopped worrying about that, and about who else she might have gotten into her bed if she hadn't run into me. Just glad it was me she had seen on that stretch of Inverness beach and called out 'Hallo!' to.

I woke at my usual pre-dawn hour, after not enough sleep, and began to fret about what to do with myself for the next few hours. Suzanne solved the problem by squirming sleepily into my arms and we began to play again. The next time I opened my eyes it was broad daylight and Suzanne, naked and beautiful as Sheba, was sitting on the edge of the bed, a cup of tea in her hand.

"For you, sleepy head. I thought you said you wake up early!"

"I don't usually get such wholesome exercise," I said, taking the tea, suddenly shy. She gave it to me with a kiss, her breast falling softly against my neck where it fitted nicely into a hollow there under my jaw.

"I'm going to spill this tea," I muttered.

She took the cup from me.

I said in a while, "If you'd played Tony Perkins, the movie would've ended differently."

"If I'd played Tony Perkins," she replied, "there wouldn't have been a movie."

I showered in her room. Then I began to worry that she hadn't said anything about her plans, about how we were to see each other again. I suddenly realized that, after all, I had been nothing but a distraction for her, just as I had feared and had determined not to be.

At the door, she turned and said, "Are you familiar with Antigonish?"

"No."

"You okay?"

"Yes," I said woodenly.

"You don't seem okay."

She had emerged from her bath earlier with her hair once again in captivity, wearing, besides those black-framed glasses, a severely tailored skirt and a blouse with full sleeves and a big bow at the neck. When she paused at the door and turned to face me, the bow grazed my jaw. I said irritably, "I'm okay, I hate that blouse."

"Ooh! A little case of the PCDs?"

"PCDs?"

"Post-coital depression?"

She palmed the bow flat and kissed my jaw on the spot where it had touched.

"Is that better?" she asked.

"Almost as good as flowers," I snapped.

"Oh, oh! I get it. Hey! I don't intend to let you get away." She opened the door and walked out into the brilliant sunlight, harsh as reality. "Did you think," she asked over her shoulder, "it was an accident? Our meeting on the beach like that yesterday?"

Before I could think of any answer but "yeah," she was in her car. She rolled down the window to call, "Brigid, be a dear and take my key to the desk, too, would you? I'll meet you at the Coady Institute. St. F.X. The last exit for Antigonish. You can't miss it. I'll be in the library. Sister Marie Joseph can find me." Then she was gone.

What did she mean did I think it was an accident meeting her on the beach? What else could it have been?

Chapter 8

How could our meeting have been anything but accidental?

I worried this question the way a cat worries a mouse. All the way to Antigonish. Sometimes I pretended to think about something else, but then the question would stir and I would pummel it again. But, however hard I pounced, the question remained alive and well, playing with me, not I with it.

As everyone had assured me, finding St. Francis Xavier University was no problem. I asked the first person I saw to point out the Coady Institute.

Suzanne was driving a blue Ford Escort. My first premonition of trouble came when I did not see it among the half dozen cars parked in the Coady parking lot. I walked round to the library and asked for Sister Mary Joseph.

"Oh, Sister Donovan! I have terrible news." Sister Mary Joseph was small and dark, her habit white. She milked her hands in agitation, looking up into my eyes, the anxiety in her own magnified by heavy lenses.

"Was she hurt?" I cried, imagining an auto accident. Imagining Suzanne a smear of blood and broken bones.

"We don't know," whispered Sister Mary Joseph. "We are praying," she added, as if to reassure me: All bases have been covered, everything possible is being done.

"Where is she?" I whispered too. Urgently. Desperately hoping the answer would be the name of a hospital, not directions to the morgue. "I would like to see her." I hesitated, contemplating the worst. "If I could."

Sister Mary Joseph had moved back a step, away from me, alarm replacing the concern her eyes had so recently held. "But of course we don't know where she is," she said.

"Say what!" I cried.

Someone hissed, "Shhh!"

Sister Mary Joseph appeared to be on the verge of tears. "There!" she said, right out loud. "I've made a muddle of things again!" She turned and scuttled away through a door behind the desk, leaving me feeling frantic, still imagining Suzanne dead or dying.

"Sister Mary Joseph!" I cried after her. "Wait!"

"Shhh! Please!" said an African woman wearing a brightly printed muu muu and a severe expression.

Sister Mary Joseph materialized at my elbow clutching a handful of pink memos. "You have several messages," she said. "You can use the phone in the office. Follow me."

The pink notes were records of phone calls to me. The ones with area code 207 were from Pearl MacDonald, Sister Pat, and Sister Barnabas. The others were Nova Scotia numbers: Faith MacDonald, Mrs. Pearl MacDonald, and Sister Marie of the orphanage in Halifax. On a sheet of yellow foolscap, boldly scrawled, was a note from Suzanne. I read it first.

"Sorry I'm missing you. Julie's disappeared. I'm off to Halifax. Call me—454-6734." At the bottom of the sheet, discreetly printed, was the question, "How do you like your eggs?"

"Sister Donovan?"

I realized Sister Mary Joseph had been coughing to catch my attention. "I'm not a Sister," I growled.

"Yes, Sister," she said, head bobbing in eternal acquiescence. "I'll leave you to your privacy," she whispered. "And don't worry about the charges. Sister MacDonald said. I'll be out at the desk if you need me."

I called Sister Pat first and got Barney. Some days are like that. I said, "Let me speak to Pat."

"You're just the person I want to talk to," Barney replied.

"Something dreadful has happened."

In the background I could hear Pat call, "If that's Brigid, let me talk with her."

I said again, "Barney, put Pat on."

I heard what sounded like a struggle at the other end of the line. I cried out, "Pat! is that you?"

"Brigid!" I heard faintly. It was Pat. And then, "I told you I wanted to talk with her first!" This is not like you." Finally, "Well, it's *very* like you!" followed by a crash and silence. A moment later I heard a door slam. The next voice I heard would belong to the victor. My good humor, lost in the parking lot behind Coady, was suddenly restored.

"Brigid!" cried Pat, "Who the devil is this Compton woman!"

I remembered: Once before Pat had seemed jealous. With some reason then, too. "She's Julie's cousin," I said, biting back a laugh. "Why?"

"Where'd you meet her?"

"In church. Why?" I asked again.

"She called here. How'd she get this number?" Before I could suggest that she had probably talked with Pearl MacDonald, Pat rushed on. "She said she wanted to know how you like your eggs for breakfast! Brigid, what is going on?"

Mind you, it's not like there could ever be anything going on between Pat and me. Buried in a police file in Manhattan is the suggestion that Sister Pat and I are honeys, a circumstance Pat has made clear she regards as worse than death.

"Did you tell her," I asked, "that I prefer chevron with basil to eggs?"

That seemed to calm her down some. She said, after a moment's pause, "Have you heard about Julie?"

"No. I think that's why I'm calling."

Julie had been abducted some time the day before by Crazy Arthur, or Jesus, as he preferred to be called.

"Why would he do that?" I asked, puzzled. It wasn't in the script, or—since it was Arthur—not in the Scriptures. Perhaps Arthur, like Hamlet, was but mad north-northwest.

"For ransom." Pat seemed surprised at my question.

"Ransom? Arthur? Are you serious?"

"I've seen the ransom note."

"What does it say?"

"The usual."

"Pat, be real. What's usual about ransom notes?"

"Brigid, why are you being so difficult? The note said, uh, I wrote it down. 'I have Julie. Though her price is far above rubies, for her safe return, the price is only $1,000,000. You have two days to get it together.'"

I mulled it over; it was Sister McDonald's dime. The biblical quote sounded like Arthur, though the Biblical reference to rubies about a woman of virtue didn't seem apt for Julie. Easy virtue maybe. And there was humor that did not seem like the intense young man I had briefly seen at Shangri-La. I remembered the crazy blue eyes boring into mine when the Christ-like figure said, "Forgive them, father, they know not what they do."

"Brigid? Are you there?"

"Yeah. I was just thinking. Who got the note?"

"Pearl. She wants to talk with you."

"I know. I guess I better call her."

"Brigid? When are you coming home?"

"Home? You mean to Greenville?"

"I mean here!" she said irritably. "I put down your floor joists yesterday."

"*My* floor joists? We don't have approval from the planning board."

"I'm adding a room to the milking shed, so it's none of their business."

"I'm going to live with Rosie?"

"No, Rosie and I can get along another winter in with the chickens. Brigid, when are you coming home?"

"I'll get back to you after I call Pearl."

I hung up, cutting her off as she said, "Brigid!" in a voice that reminded me of Mother's—as in Mother Superior. Like I've said many times before, scratch a Nun, find a bully. Still, it was nice, this evidence that she cared. Pearl MacDonald was next. She answered the phone herself.

"Pearl MacDonald, here. Can I help you?"

"Hi. Brigid Donovan."

"I thought it might be you. Have you spoken with Suzanne?"

On an inspiration I ventured, "She didn't intercept me until last night at Inverness."

Pearl's silence was short but perceptible and told me what I wanted to know. Been afraid to find out. Suzanne did set me up. Because Pearl had told her to. It hadn't been my silver locks and elusive beauty after all that had attracted her.

Pearl said breezily, "I meant, have you called her yet in Halifax?"

I said, "She couldn't possibly have gotten to Halifax yet. I just got to Antigonish myself. She was only ten or fifteen minutes ahead of me."

"Then you don't know."

"Well, I know Julie's missing. And Arthur."

"Not missing exactly."

I saw no point in arguing, not even on Sister MacDonald's dime. I waited.

"Arthur kidnapped her."

"So Pat said."

"You seem skeptical."

"The note didn't sound like Arthur. It sounded more like something Arjuna might have cooked up."

This pause was longer. Then Pearl said, "You never met Arjuna."

"No," I agreed. "But I saw his picture. And I think Julie's stigmata was Arjuna's idea. He seemed..." I cast about for a good word, and settled on frivolous. "Arthur isn't frivolous," I observed.

"No, you're right. Arthur's not. That's why I'm so worried."

"But if it's a hoax?"

"Oh, it's no hoax. I've spoken to Arthur." Her voice broke, and then she continued steadily, "He said, I have it written down, 'I had rather be a toad than keep a corner on the thing I love for another's use.'"

"He said that?"

"You know how he talks."

"Still. That's not the Bible. Anyway, I don't get it. Pat said he left a ransom note praising her virtue."

"Well, he did. But, this morning when I spoke with him, he said if we wanted to see—he called her 'the strumpet'. He said if we wanted to see her alive it would cost $1,000,000."

"Well," I said, "his price hasn't changed. What do you want me to do?"

"The police think the call came from Nova Scotia. If you will get in touch with Suzanne, she has my instructions. The family wishes to hire you, Brigid. You come highly recommended."

That was gratifying. I wondered who had done the recommending. I said, "Explain to me about Suzanne."

Another silence, then, "You'll have to ask Suzanne for explanations. She exceeded my instructions. Lavishly exceeded them."

The next sound I heard was a dial tone.

No one answered the phone in Scotsburn. I guessed that Faith and Hope were out in the barn. No answer in Smelts Brook either. That puzzled me, but then I decided Mrs. MacDonald must have taken a load of crafts up to Lauraine's in Neil's Harbour. I wondered how she got to and fro. I hadn't seen a car. I looked at my watch. Still only 9:45. I shook my wrist and listened to the tick. It was running, but it felt like tomorrow morning. I decided to hit the road for Halifax. I could stop at the orphanage and talk to Sister Marie in person. And I could call Suzanne from there. She would be home by then.

Thinking of calling Suzanne from the luxury of Mother Superior's office brought another thought in train. I realized that the family who had taken an interest in Eddie MacDonald, Pearl MacDonald's baby, was none other than Suzanne's family. I could hear Mother Superior as she intoned, piously, "The Comptons, one of our better Halifax families." You bet they took an interest, I thought. He was one of them. What I didn't know is how good, let alone best, that made them.

Chapter 9

The tone of Arthur's second message worried me. Worried me for more than one reason, though I could put my finger on only one. There was nothing Biblical in his "I had rather be a toad" message. But, if it wasn't from the Bible, where did it come from, I wondered. Each time I posed that question it touched off a tremor of terror in me. I seemed to know the quote, but I couldn't place it. Couldn't seem to think of the right context for it.

I tried letting the problem alone, hoping my unreliable gray cells would reactivate. But I arrived at the convent of St. Therese with nothing stirring among them but dread. The dread by then had become familiar and I believed, as Pearl seemed to, that Julie was in great danger.

Seeing her in danger subtly changed my perception of her. Pity, I guess, does that. In place of the willful, schizophrenic manipulator I had instinctively disliked, I saw a naughty, childlike girl whom I cared for. Posturing that before had seemed to be little short of criminal, I had come to regard as Julie's dauntlessness and non-conformity. An independence of spirit. The thought of what crazy Arthur might do to cut that independence short, to exact obedience, to make Julie thoroughly his, filled me with dread. I thought of Othello on stage, maddened by Iago, cutting off Desdemona's life in the softness of a pillow, as he murdered, sobbing, "Baccio." Kiss.

The light came on as I pulled into the parking lot of the St.

Therese orphanage alongside an acre or two of freshly planted impatiens. That last quote, the one about the toad, I was suddenly sure came from Othello. The little gray cells never let you down, I exalted.

But my joy of recognition was immediately subdued by the implication of what I'd discovered. I doubted Arthur would redeem his honor with cash. And I doubted he would be so gentle as the warrior Othello in exacting retribution from Julie for being, in his words, a strumpet. I remembered with foreboding the usage adulterous women in the Bible received. They were stoned to death. I took small comfort from the fact that Jesus once had refused to exact such a punishment; Jesus' Father condoned it. Condoned that and worse. And it was the father, not the son, whom Arthur/Jesus had cited the one time I met him, looking crazy, thinking he was the Son of God.

At the orphanage they suggested I'd find Sister Marie in the kitchen. She was glad to see me and she, too, was quite agitated about Julie. "Such a beautiful child," she said. Apparently the Comptons had brought Julie to the convent often to visit.

"Mother was called away," Sister Marie explained. "She will be sorry to have missed you."

Marie had been cutting carrots when I found her. The young woman who prepped had called in sick. "She said the flu!" Sister Marie sniffed. "Odd flu I'd say, lasts till early afternoon, and you get it once every six or seven days!"

"Hangover?"

But the nun only glowered. Keeping her ill-speaking down to a venial sin, apparently. She told me that Sister Agnes, Mother Superior, had called Eskasoni to find me, and then Antigonish. "You're to call Sister MacDonald in Maine right away," she said, then added, "Reverse the charges."

I explained that I already had called 'Sister' MacDonald, but that I'd still like to use the phone. "A local number," I reassured her.

Sister Marie pulled the large white apron over her head and patted down the stiff black skirt of her habit. I followed her down the echoing corridors, between somber oil portraits of women in black and men in scarlet. There was only one I liked: Saint Theresa writhing orgasmically on a shaft of light from heaven.

Suzanne answered on the first ring.

"Brigid, thank God! Where've you been?"

"Talking on the phone."

"Let me tell you how to get here."

"Whoah!" I said. "I have a couple issues with you." One especially, I thought, longing to be reassured. I let the silence between us lengthen. I was afraid to ask my question: "Were you just using me?"

Finally Suzanne said, "You haven't spoken with Pearl yet?"

I said, "Yeah. I talked to Pearl."

"Didn't she hire you? To find Julie?"

Another silence as I gathered my courage. "About our meeting…there, on the beach. At Inverness." I didn't wait for her to answer. But then I hadn't asked a question, really. Abruptly I said, "It's like a tango, hiring someone, it takes two to make a contract."

"Oh, Brigid!"

"What do you mean 'Oh, Brigid!'? Oh Suzanne! is more like it."

"Don't be prickly, dear, I couldn't bear it. And who is that Pat woman? You should have told me there was someone in your life."

I started to laugh. "There isn't, really." Deciding to accept the balance Suzanne had struck. "Okay, how do I get to your place?"

She directed me: across the Angus MacDonald Bridge, take the first right, then the second left. "Weston Street. Number 1980. You can't miss it. If you get lost, ask someone for the street where all the Dykes live." She was laughing as she hung up. She has a nice laugh, kind of hearty, not like people who get tenure.

She was right about the house being easy to find. Her apartment was a floor-through, first story. First story U.S., not Canadian. The back opened out onto a little garden. She suggested we have tea out there. But first she wanted a kiss and that took a little while. Thinking it might be our last, I was in no hurry to cut it short.

I knew immediately when Suzanne began to lie to me. She refused to meet my eyes. She started to fuss with the tea pot, she wiped the table twice, she hung and then hung again the dish towel she had used to wipe our tea cups with.

What started her lying was my asking, "What's this about Pearl setting me up? Our meeting on the beach, it wasn't an accident. What was that all about?"

Suzanne, suddenly busy at the stove, said over her shoulder, "Pearl asked me to be on the look-out for you. Give you a hand? You know. Like if you called me."

"On the look-out? In the church at Eskasoni? On the beach at Inverness?"

From her preoccupation with tea towels, Suzanne said in an absent-minded sort of way, "She just said you were coming, you were doing a job for her. Would I assist you."

"Assist me? Assist me how?"

From the depths of her fridge, Suzanne's voice echoed coolly, "Oh, you know. She said you were investigating her. If you needed help."

"In other words, if I started to get close to something, like for instance her relationship with you? Maybe you were to assist my butt out of here?"

"Oh, Brigid! " she said, her nose in a carton of milk. Sniffing. "We may have to go out. Unless you drink your tea black."

I reached for the carton. We sniffed together. I started to say I thought it was only the spout smelling bad, but as I started to form the words my lips got tangled up in hers. Somehow Suzanne managed to set the carton safely on the counter, and somehow she managed to maneuver me safely down the hall to the bedroom.

Her bed lay in a bow window, like a garden in sun light, flowers on the window ledge, and in baskets hanging over us. Her lovemaking was exuberant. Like a kitten at play, she frolicked and teased. But her tongue was smooth as silk and wise as a cat with nine lives.

Much later we had our tea in bed. I was right, the milk, wasn't sour. Suzanne said she knew that.

I still felt wary of her. I said she didn't look like Greta Garbo, exactly, but I still got Mata Hari vibes from her. She laughed.

"Oh, Brigid," she said. "Let's see. I think I better tell you all about it."

"Sounds good to me."

"Julie's being kidnaped has changed everything," she began. The memory of Julie made her somber. She leaned out of bed and fished up a handful of clothes from the floor. She talked as she sorted through them, handing mine to me, and beginning to put on her own.

"When Pearl called to warn me about you, she was afraid you might cotton to her connection with us. For lots of reasons she didn't want that to happen. So, she suggested I meet up with you, keep an eye on you, and…well, redirect your attention if that became necessary."

"So, Eskasoni wasn't an accident."

"Eskasoni was easy, and no, it wasn't an accident. Inverness was trickier." She threw back her head and laughed, that hearty, untenured laugh I had grown so fond of. "I thought for sure you'd notice me at those lay-bys. I stopped every time you did."

I thought back on my trip from Smelt Brook to the end of the Cabot Trail. "I guess I was too nervous about the drop-off to notice anyone."

"Scared of heights?"

I admitted it. I asked how she'd managed the 'chance' encounter on the beach.

"It really wasn't hard. When I saw you stop at the motel, I waited and checked in after you. I watched. You drove away and I followed. When you turned off to the beach, I drove to the next turn-off and walked back up to meet you."

It was the next part that worried me and I didn't know how to ask. Was afraid, I guess, of the answer.

Suzanne reached over, cupped my face in her hands. I looked up at the basket of purple gloxinia hanging above her head. My eyes began to smart. Staring at the color purple, I guess, but I was unable to look away.

"Brigid," she soothed. "I'm not a Mata Hari. Though I have been told I resemble Greta Garbo."

"The hair," I said. "The hair's different." I managed a laugh.

Suzanne hadn't answered my unspoken question—why had

she made love to me?—but she had salvaged my ego. And I realized I had to be content with that.

"Yeah, the hair." She stood and pulled on her trousers. "Let's go back to the kitchen," she said. "I have to do some stuff for supper." As I started to protest, she turned and put a finger on my lips. "Don't worry, I'm going to tell you the whole story ."

The whole story was that Pearl didn't want anyone in Maine to know about her ties to the wealthy Compton family of Halifax, Nova Scotia. When I asked why, Suzanne shrugged and said something about foundations preferring to give money to poor folk.

"But when you went to Scotsburn and discovered Hope and Charity, that tore it," Suzanne said. "I talked to Pearl after I met you at Eskasoni. Faith had already called her. Pearl said I could go home, any interference from me at that point, she said, would just make you suspicious. So...."

She dropped the potato she had been peeling and came over to the table where I sat. She bent over me. Her tongue darted briefly into the hollow of my ear, then she whispered. "So Inverness had nothing to do with Pearl, or the investigation. Satisfied?"

" Yeah," I said. Happily.

"What you don't know," Suzanne resumed, picking up the half-peeled potato, "is that my uncle, Arjuna, was Eddie MacDonald's father."

I worked it out in stages. Suzanne puttering silently at the sink, gave me all the time I needed.

First, this man Arjuna, well loved by Suzanne—and by Pearl—was a rapist. Didn't make sense. I said, "I saw a picture of Arjuna. Never met him. He didn't strike me as a rapist. I guess you can never tell."

"Pearl told you she was raped?" Suzanne didn't sound very interested. I said yes she had.

"I guess, technically, that's what it was. She was only sixteen. She worked for us. Before I was born. They were both just a couple of kids, Dave—that's Arjuna—he was only eighteen. But he was of age. I guess Pearl could call it rape. The way I heard the story no one wanted a marriage, Pearl least of all.

"Do you like french fries?" she asked.

"Yeah, love 'em."

"As you probably gathered from Sister Agnes, the Comptons are one of Halifax's 'leading families.'" She turned, a large bottle of oil in her hand, and dropped me a curtsy. "My grandparents used to hire a lot of the orphans—their first jobs. They assumed responsibility for Eddie, without acknowledging him. Sent him to Dalhousie, and then to Pratt in New York City."

Next stage of my reasoning was from Eddie to Julie. Eddie MacDonald was Julie's father. Pearl MacDonald, Julie's grandmother. That seemed to make Arjuna Julie's grandfather.

"Was Arjuna Julie's grandfather?" I asked.

Gloomily, Suzanne replied, "Yes. He was."

"Did you know...," I started to ask.

"About their affair? I loved him, but Arjuna was a rascal."

"Did Julie know?"

"Oh, I imagine so. It wouldn't be like either Pearl or Arjuna to keep it from her."

I thought about it. Julie claiming that Pearl was jealous. I could imagine the scenes, the two willful women, Julie and her grandmother Pearl, alike in their determination, fighting over Arjuna.

I thought of Barney. I was sure she had wanted me to discover some dirt she suspected concerning Arjuna. Had she reason to think that his affair with Julie was incestuous? That would be a scandal worth blackmail. The temple, with its condominiums, all that tourist trade. We were talking big money. An affair between the 'celibate' monk and his granddaughter would put paid to the whole scheme.

"What about Arthur?" I asked.

"Arthur?"

"Pearl calls him Jesus. I guess he calls himself Jesus."

"The one who kidnaped Julie. What about him?"

"I wonder whether he knew. That Arjuna was Julie's grandfather."

"Oh, God! I hope not. He's very crazy."

There seemed to be a lot of motives in all of this for murder: envy, jealousy, delusion, and now the fate of the temple housing development, and that meant megabucks.

Just then the phone rang. Suzanne answered it in the hall. She mostly listened, and when she responded, her back was turned, her voice low. I couldn't have overheard if I tried. I know, because I did try. After a few moments, Suzanne turned to me, her hand over the mouthpiece. She looked worried.

"It's Pearl," she said. "For you."

Chapter 10

"What are you doing at Suzanne's?" a peevish voice inquired. I knew it was Pearl, but it sounded like Pat. My heart lurched to a full stop.

"Nothing," my dutiful lips responded. But my errant brain began to amuse itself, images of what I had been doing at Suzanne's flooding its remnant cells.

"I expected," said Pearl at her most peremptory, "that you would be working to find Julie. You don't seem to appreciate the seriousness of the matter."

"I can tell you who Arthur was quoting," I said brightly. "In the second ransom message. At least I'm pretty sure."

Scorn oozed out the receiver, "You believe you can identify the quote. That should be very helpful—at a Memorial Service."

"Hey!" I said. "I never agreed to work on this case."

"That wasn't my understanding."

"What would you like me to be doing?"

"I want you back here. Before the trail is entirely cold." Then she added, with crisp authority, "I want my van parked in my door-yard by eight tomorrow morning!"

Suzanne raged at Pearl, calling her a bully, which she certainly was. But I insisted on going. Not because of the bullying, but because Pearl was right that Julie was in danger. And if I stayed in Halifax I wouldn't be on the case, I'd be in bed. She was also right that I should begin the search where the abduction occurred.

"I can't believe," Suzanne shouted when she saw that I really meant to leave, "that you'd be so wimpy as to do what Pearl tells you. My God, Pearl says 'Jump!' to anyone, and they ask 'How high?' I suppose you intend to be there by eight?"

"Yeah."

"You could at least stay for dinner."

I tried to chuckle, a woman-in-control-of-every-situation kind of a chuckle, wry and worldly. It came out a squawk. I said, "If I stayed for dinner, Suzanne, you know as well as I do where we'd have dessert."

As I ran down the outside steps she wailed from the doorway, "I still don't know how you like your eggs!"

"Sunny side up!" I yelled, rolling past her door. I threw her a kiss. In the rear view mirror I saw her throw one back. Maybe I was forgiven.

It was about forty miles out of my way, but I decided to detour up to Scotsburn and check things out with Faith and Hope, Pearl MacDonald's sisters. They had left that message for me in Antigonish, and I had never spoken with them. Nor with their mother in Smelt Brook. I suddenly started to worry about all three of them. To worry about them and be angry with myself. Angry and guilty. Julie was in serious danger. Either that or beyond help. And I had spent my afternoon playing.

That's when I realized that what I wanted more than anything in the world was a frosty bottle of Labatt beer. It used to be my favorite. Well, after Ringnes it was my favorite.

I didn't have a Nova Scotia AA Meeting Book with me. I'd stopped carrying them a year or two before. Didn't figure I needed meetings any more.

But I needed a meeting then. Bad. Trying to reflect, I dredged up the old AA slogan HALT. Hungry, Angry, Lonely, Tired. Four ingredients for a terrific drunk. And I had them all—in spades.

Very hungry, I realized, and leaving behind in the oven at 1980 Weston Street a wonderful smelling moussaka.

Angry. With myself. With Pearl for jerking my strings. At Suzanne for jerking them, too. Or jangling them.

Lonely, very lonely. Lonely for Suzanne. Lonely, I realized, for Pat. Being lonely for Pat was a terminal loneliness.

And tired. I tried to remember whether if when I was younger I could make love all afternoon and afterwards have any energy. I decided that when I was younger I would also have been drunk. In any case, I couldn't remember.

I stopped at the next Irving Restaurant and ordered Brunswick Stew. It wasn't bad, but it wasn't moussaka. I had pie and ice cream for dessert. To take care of my sugar craving; read 'alcohol'.

I drove into the door-yard of the Scotsburn farm not long after sunset. I thought I saw a light in a window high up in the barn. It seemed an odd place for the sisters to be at that hour, a little after ten. But, starting toward the barn, I looked up again, and it had disappeared. The moon, which was nearly full and bright, had risen into a bank of clouds. I decided the light in the window had been a reflection of the rising moon.

Faith and Hope were puttering busily in the kitchen when I entered, Faith sterilizing the milking equipment, Hope spinning. The room smelled cosy, of wood smoke and spices. I wondered what they had had for supper.

They didn't seem surprised to see me. "We thought, when you didn't call, Mrs. Donovan, that you might stop by," Faith began.

"We're usually in bed by now," Hope continued in a wistful voice.

"Sorry to be so late. I was in Halifax. Interviewing Suzanne Compton." I felt a blush warm my ears.

"Suzanne. Such a sweet girl. So intelligent," the sisters murmured.

"Have you heard anything more about Julie?" I asked. Together they denied that they had. They seemed calmer than I expected them to be. "You don't seem very upset," I ventured.

Hope began to cry. Faith hurried over to her, wiping her hands on her apron as she went. The sisters rocked back and forth together. It was hard to tell who was comforting whom, they looked so alike, both with hair pulled back tight into tidy buns,

72

both in cotton print dresses, black oxfords, ragged cardigans and big white aprons. It was Hope who broke their embrace. She said, "Forgive us, Mrs. Donovan."

Faith offered to make some tea. I said never mind, it was past their bed time. I asked whether they had spoken with their mother in Smelt Brook.

"Not since this morning," said Faith.

"Not exactly," said Hope, and then she began to busy herself at the spinning wheel again.

"She means," explained Faith, "we haven't spoken with Mother since the kidnaping."

Hope let out a sob.

"I must go," I said. "Sorry I disturbed you."

Faith assured me I had not disturbed them. She said she knew I must hurry back to Maine and get on the trail of Arthur and Julie. "We worry so about Arthur, I do hate to call him Jesus."

"Yeah, well." I thought it was probably typical of Faith to worry more about the perpetrator of a crime than about the victim. I asked whether she had talked with Pearl. Told her Pearl had hired me.

Faith looked embarrassed. "She said to tell you…. It was something about the van," she finished lamely.

"To get it there to Xanadu by eight in the morning," exclaimed Hope acidly.

When I left I looked up at the barn. The moon, risen now above the clouds, washed it in a milky light. The windows all were dark. I wondered again at the light I had seen earlier and again dismissed it. I reflected on the sisters' being up so late and their cautious responses to my questions, their apparent calmness when I expected them to be beside themselves with worry. They were exhausted, I decided. Like me.

At the highway I hung a left and headed toward Cape Breton. I never have figured out exactly why I did. Some combination of things: Hope's 'not exactly' when I asked if they'd talked to their mother; and, probably, because I still smarted from Suzanne calling me a wimp. Defying Pearl for whatever reason felt like balm on my ego.

I didn't get far that night, just to Antigonish where I stopped at a little motel on the highway. Drifting off to sleep, I imagined Pearl's face, looking out her window next morning at eight and no van. Prelude to happy dreams. Whoever in the dream I made love with all night—I never was sure whether it was Pat or Suzanne—she thought I was awesome.

They took plastic at the motel, but I needed to find someplace cheap for breakfast, my roll of pretty Canadian paper was getting thin. My clothes needed some thinking about, too. Another night on the road meant I'd have to recycle them for the third time. And none of what I'd brought looked too wonderful to begin with. Maybe on my return I would stop in Antigonish to do a laundry, or pick up a new shirt. If I could find a thrift, I might splurge and get a whole new outfit.

Oatmeal and brown toast for breakfast and I was on my way. Crossing the Canso Causeway in the early morning light was like entering a Chinese landscape painting, hills lost in mist, sea birds lounging against a pale gray sky. I was content with the world, pleased at my decision to defy Pearl, happy with the thought that soon I would be rocking in sweet companionship with Mrs. MacDonald. I wondered what she would offer me this time for tea.

As I entered Cape Breton Highlands National Park and began to maneuver those curves, skirting those precipitous drops, my mood became somber. I began to contemplate the tangled relationships I had uncovered and the many motives people had had for destroying Arjuna.

Julie's claim that Pearl, because of jealousy and envy, wanted to get rid of her, no longer seemed so absurd. I toyed with the possibility that Pearl was somehow behind this kidnaping of Julie by the schizophrenic Arthur. But it didn't play.

What played better, now that I knew more, was that Pearl might have killed Arjuna. I knew from experience, my own and other people's, how stinking thinking indulged in year after year can warp a person's reason. If Pearl had come to believe that her adolescent encounter with Arjuna really had been rape, and that he had abandoned her, no matter how much she cared for him,

74

she could have done him harm. I remembered the look of her as she held Arjuna's photo that morning in her office after he died. Othello flashed again through my mind. People kill from love as well as from hate. As for the method of his dying: Pearl, if she were crazy enough, might have ritualized Arjuna's killing, deliberately killing him as she had killed her violent, violating father when she was a girl.

But if madness and delusion were the key, then the most likely suspect would have to be Arthur. He almost certainly had kidnapped Julie and intended her harm. He certainly had known that Arjuna and Julie were living together at Shangri-La. That in itself could be sufficient reason for him to punish Julie, his motives a combination of jealousy and righteousness. And, I saw now, Julie's affair might have prompted him first to kill Arjuna. But the method puzzled me. Fire might seem like divine retribution. But tying Arjuna to his bed, as old man MacDonald had been tied in his? That was stretching coincidence too far.

Then there was the question of money. Money seemed to me to have been a motive from the start; the lack of it on my part and the extravagant abundance of it everywhere else: at Shangri-La, at the Convent of St. Therese, in the Compton family. Through my new playmate, Suzanne Compton, I had become aware that money might have motivated whoever murdered Arjuna. The rascally monk who was not only not celibate, but having an affair with his own granddaughter. That would not go over in Soperton, Maine. I remembered Pat's disgust at what she called his hypocrisy. And Pat had called Arjuna's affair with Julie 'small beer.' That, of course, was before she knew of the incest. She had meant that Arjuna was also seeing men; and that, perhaps, opened another whole world of motives I had not even begun to imagine. As I wondered who it might have been, the image of Arthur/Jesus rose in my mind, the long silky blond hair, the even features, the tall graceful body. Arjuna and Jesus. It was so bizarre I had to laugh.

Well, there were motives a-plenty. But if solutions were arrived at by democratic methods, crazy Arthur would win. With a spurt of adrenaline disguised as anxiety, I knew I had to find

Julie. Why, I wondered, did I think Mrs. MacDonald could help? Maybe because I was sure she could never lie to me. Not even by omission.

Shortly before noon I arrived at Neil Harbour and headed down the dirt road to Mrs. MacDonald's tiny house. The sea was tranquil, the air warm. The fog had finally burned off leaving the world looking crisp, fresh off the press, the dirge of fog horns ousted by ragtime gulls skittering along the shore. I happily anticipated my tea.

No one answered my knock. I rattled both the door and the windows, and called her name. Peering through the window and the filmy curtains, I imagined I could see her, as I had two days before, busy at the counter kneading bread.

Off to Laurraine's I decided. Not to worry, though; it wouldn't hurt to stretch my legs some. I wandered off toward the shore.

My stomach's demand for attention finally brought me back to the little house. I was sure Mrs. MacDonald had not returned, but I went through a routine of rattling and shouting anyway.

There was a take-out down the road about half an hour. An angry squawk from my stomach, peremptory as an order from Pearl MacDonald, cut short my internal debate, and I returned to my car. If old Mrs. MacDonald still wasn't here when I came back, I thought, well I'd do something then to find her.

Greasy cheeseburger, greasy French fries and, to top off my cholesterol extravaganza, a chocolate shake. Mmm Mmm, good! Burping contentedly I bounced down the dirt road to the little house shortly after one. Still no Mrs. MacDonald!

A new discontent had come to afflict me. I should have used the rest room at the take-out. I looked around at my options. The beach was cobblestone and rather flat. Too cold, also, to go out wading. The wind-swept headland was bare of trees or shrubs, the two other houses in full view, one on each side. And, while there wasn't much traffic, an occasional car did pass down the road in front.

Circling the house looking for a private spot, I saw in back exactly what I needed. An outhouse. I should have known. A rush of affection warmed me. She was so hardy, had survived so much, lived so simply, and at ninety-some was still so open to life, so acute, so.... So perfect. I decided I was in love.

I noticed the odor as I drew near the door. Not the ordinary smell of an outhouse, which if you're used to it, smells basic rather than bad. This was a sickening smell, one you wanted to avoid. I covered my nose and mouth with a tissue thinking Mrs. MacDonald must store garbage in there, away from raccoons. I thought some scraps of meat must have started to rot.

She was sitting propped on the bench, looking blankly out at me. A million flies had settled on the blood that had gushed from her breast, settled on her staring eyes.

I vomited at her feet.

Chapter 11

I don't know how long I tried to clean vomit off the sensible black oxfords with their neatly tied bows. With handfuls of new spring grass I scoured and scoured.

Cold brought me to my senses. The sun had disappeared behind a bank of darkening clouds, a sharp wind blew off the sea. Wiping my hands on my trousers, my mouth on my sleeve, I walked stiffly across to the neighbor's next door. Not in. Nor the family on the other side. I thought, giddily, that I might as well pee, and I did, by the back door of her house, her blank eyes my only witness.

The back door was unlocked. Beyond a narrow entry where broom, mop, dust pan and bucket were neatly stored, was her bedroom. Sparely furnished, austere as she herself had been, the room held a small white metal bed, a bureau and a bedside table. The only spots of color were a red Bible with a gold cross, and a crazy quilt patterned with scraps from bright summer dresses. The phone sat between Bible and lamp on the bedside table.

The operator said to hold tight, someone would be with me shortly. Shortly was close to half an hour. I retreated to the front room and amused myself looking through the photo albums Mrs. MacDonald had brought out to show me. The one on top was open. Julie's pretty face, adolescent and innocent, smiled from a dozen photos. Whatever happened must have started right after I left, Mrs. MacDonald wasn't one to leave things out. She had had time to rinse our dishes, but not to put away the albums.

The Mountie, when he finally arrived, was a disappointment, about my age, dressed in khaki gray, and driving a little Japanese car. They apparently hadn't taken my phone call seriously. He became suddenly efficient, though, after following me out and seeing her there on the outhouse bench. Ten minutes later the yard in front held half a dozen cars and most of the people who lived in Smelt Brook. I recognized the secretary from the fish plant. She hurried over to me.

"Remember me?" she said, taking my elbow. I didn't resist. I needed taking in hand.

"Yeah, I do."

"God, what a shock! Come with me. I'll fix you some tea. It'll be forever before they need you." She called to the man who seemed to have taken charge, "Jason! I'm taking Mrs...." She looked at me inquiringly.

"Donovan. Brigid Donovan."

"Mrs. Donovan with me."

He tipped his finger at her and half smiled.

"He's my cousin," she confided, pulling me along behind her out to the road. "I'm just two houses down," she said.

Her name was Helen. Helen Burns. She made us tea, and she made us toast. Her house shared with Mrs. MacDonald's an uncompromising aesthetic, a Shaker-like simplicity though it was larger. Arranged in geometric order on one wall were family photos, several of children.

"Yours?" I nodded at them.

"Yes," she said. "Four boys."

"They're very tidy."

She poured our tea. "Have to be," she observed. "So little room. Not like in Usa."

"Usa?"

"Where you come from."

She didn't seem hostile. And Usa, I guess, is better than America. Politically better. But I didn't think it would play in Peoria. I laughed a little. She made soothing noises.

We sat a while in silence. On my second cup of tea, I began to feel more normal, less light-headed, less like I was in a bad dream, my body unresponsive to my desires, hoping I would soon wake up. She must have sensed the change, for she leaned toward me and said, "Might be a good time to make any phone calls." She nodded to a phone on the wall leading into the kitchen.

"I have a credit card."

"Not to worry," she said.

I called Suzanne. She didn't seem delighted to hear my voice. She had blown me a kiss, but she hadn't forgiven me. Tears smarted my eyes. "Suzanne," I said, "be kind. Something awful has happened."

She took charge rapidly when she heard my news. She took charge as in 'made for tenure.' Tenure and other big things. She said a lawyer would be there in Smelt Brook within the hour. How, I asked, was that possible? She said please just trust her, the Compton's firm of lawyers in Sydney would know of someone close by who was reliable. She said she would be there by evening with a lawyer from Halifax. She asked who was in charge of the investigation. I let her talk with Helen.

"You have very fancy friends," Helen observed when she hung up. Her end of the conversation had been almost entirely small sounds of assent.

"I guess," I said. "I don't know."

"Well, they are."

It may have been my imagination, but Helen seemed cooler to me somehow, more correct than warm as she had been when she rescued me. In time her cousin, who had given permission for me to leave the scene, came by.

"Jason," she said, "before you question Mrs. Donovan, come look at this tax form Reggie got in the mail and tell me what you think of it."

He looked surprised, but he followed her into the kitchen. I could hear the murmur of their voices, but not what they said. The tax form couldn't have been long or required much interpretation. They returned to the sitting room promptly. Jason's manner echoed the correctness that Helen's had assumed.

"Mrs. Donovan," he said, "Jason MacKenzie. I understand

from Helen that your lawyer will be here shortly. If you would prefer to wait for him, that is perfectly acceptable. But if you wish to tell me what happened, it would be helpful." He held a pad for taking notes diffidently in his hand.

"Sure," I said. "Whatever."

"Then I must warn you that I will take down what you say and anything that you say can be used in evidence against you."

"Say what?"

True to her word, Suzanne had a lawyer to Smelt Brook in under an hour. Helen had been right. We were talking Major League here. He arrived in a helicopter. It landed on the cobbled beach across the road.

I had already told Jason about finding the body. He said there didn't seem to be many fingerprints around and wanted to know whether they could take mine for comparison. I told him sure, but that of course mine would be everywhere, that I'd used the phone, and I'd looked through the photo albums. I said, "If you're saying someone wiped the place clean of fingerprints, it would be crazy to think that someone was me. Wouldn't it?" I added. His expression was so blank I wasn't sure he was even listening.

Suzanne's lawyer was a young man, dressed for the city and looking out of place there at land's end. He didn't quite chastise me for talking with the RCMP, but it was clear that he regarded my conduct as imprudent at best. At worst, what? Insubordination? Probably. When Suzanne arrived at dusk, on the arm of an expensive, elderly man in a three-piece suit, she said, "But Brigid! I *told* you not to talk to anyone until our lawyers arrived."

She had. What could I say?

They had flown from Halifax to Sydney, and been driven from there in a black limousine. Mr. Brougham, the Halifax lawyer, spoke briefly with Jason MacKenzie, then beckoned to Suzanne and me. I was free to go, he said. He looked inquiringly at Suzanne. She told him he had done splendidly and she was grateful. Then she said she would return to Halifax with me.

"Mrs. Donovan," she said, nodding in my direction, "after her

81

ordeal, shall need support." She offered Brougham her hand, forestalling any suggestion of his that I might be better supported by some minion. I thought of pictures I had seen of Queen Elizabeth offering her hand to men who looked like Brougham.

I went back to the house and tried to offer my hand to Helen. She seemed not to see it, but she said she was glad to have been of assistance.

"Yeah," I said.

Suzanne was already behind the wheel of the van when I returned to Mrs. MacDonald's. The black limousine and the black helicopter with their gaggle of lawyers had disappeared. So had the crowd. It was cold. The wind from off the sea blew with the bitterness of a short-changed miser, relentlessly nagging.

"I had Noel phone ahead," Suzanne called as I approached. "We have a reservation at a little motel I know about in Inverness."

That was the last friendly thing she said to me until we got there.

Climbing into the van my stomach, made comatose by all the stress, roared back to life. "Could we stop somewhere? I'm hungry," I said.

"In my bag," said Suzanne.

"Somewhere to eat."

"I know," she said, her voice delicately tinted with impatience. "You're hungry. In Antigonish, I made Noel stop. There are sandwiches and fruit.

"In my bag" she added, irritably, when I made no move to look.

I hopped to then and pulled her bag, a large leather saddle bag, onto my lap.

"I'd like one of the ham and cheese," she said.

"Yes, sir!"

She ignored my sally. "Brigid," she said, her hand out for the sandwich I was busy unwrapping, "I thought I told you not to talk to anyone until our lawyer arrived."

I said yeah and handed her a half.

"If that has a pickle in it, it's yours."

"I don't like pickles."

"Neither do I."

I adore pickles whenever I'm sane, but just then I wasn't. The half sandwich continued to lie on my passive hand a few inches from hers on the wheel.

"Brigid! I said I don't like pickles."

"I heard you. You don't like pickles, I mustn't talk until your lawyer arrives. And we can't stop for supper apparently." My vocal chords tangled with a sob. A sob or phlegm in my throat. Whatever, I shut up.

"Give me a break!" Suzanne said roughly. "No place around here is still open for supper. Noel says the Mountie read you your rights before you talked to him. Are you angry with me because I tried to protect you? Why did you call me if you didn't want my help?"

Having so recently seen nothing but my side of this spat, I found it marvelous how now I could see nothing but this reasonable view of Suzanne's. I picked the sandwich apart to inspect for pickles. No pickles. "Here," I said. "No pickles."

"Thank you."

We ate a while in silence. I don't know what Suzanne thought about. The road, probably. Keeping us on it while we flew along, too fast for the tight curves and the long drops I couldn't see, mercifully, because it was dark.

Maybe she was thinking about what a wimp she'd picked to go to bed with. An old wimp at that. Morosely I reflected on my fatal weakness for domineering women, starting with Heidi. Heidi, who had managed my life almost to a Ph.D. It had been a contest between her and my best buddy, Mr. Bottle. For all Heidi's determination, the contest had been uneven and Mr. B, inevitably, won. Heidi compensated with the twins, my two sons. Luckily for them. She kept their bedrooms ready for when they needed to bail out of a hectic home life with me. And she saw them through college.

Mr. B and I had a long relationship, too. He also ruled with an iron hand. But he never forgot his velvet glove. His seductive velvet glove.

Couldn't think about that velvety touch of my old buddy Booze. Think instead, I told myself, about the knuckle dusters the morning after. I'd been in the program a few twenty-four hours and most of the time, these days, it felt like I had it licked. Then suddenly, out of nowhere, I'd feel not so much that I needed a drink as convinced that to have one would be okay, like I could handle it. And that terrified me. Getting sober once was about all I could handle in this life. I'd watched, over the years, a few friends succumb to the notion that one drink wouldn't matter. Some had made it back. Some hadn't. I knew, without a doubt, that I never could.

"Did you get anything to drink?" My question, breaking the silence like an unexpected insult, startled us both.

"There's a flask of brandy in my bag. I'd like some, too."

Her request exploded in my unreceptive brain, fragmenting it. One small piece was willing. Another, terrified already by her driving, wanted courageously to tell her 'no'. Other pieces, flying rapidly into space, variously were afraid she wouldn't make love to me again, would grab her bag and drive with one hand, would….

"I don't think brandy's a good idea," I said. "Until we get to the motel, I mean." Wimp! I thought. Remind her you're a drunk. I knew I wouldn't.

She surprised me. "Good thinking," she said.

And for a little while our silence was more companionable. Then she said, "Brigid, I need to find out exactly what you told the RCMP."

"Not much. Just that I'd stopped by and went to use the outhouse and there she was."

"What did you say to explain your visit."

"I didn't."

She mulled that over in silence. "You must have said something," she said after a while. " It's not like people from the States just drop by in Smelt Brook." It sounded like a question.

I thought back. "Well, that woman Helen—the one who's Jason MacKenzie's cousin…."

"Who's Jason MacKenzie?"

"Who's Jason MacKenzie? Get with the program, Suzanne!

He was the Mountie in charge."

"Oh, him," said Suzanne.

She said it dismissively, the arrogance unconscious. It was, I realized, the arrogance of the ruling class, and I understood Helen's change in attitude toward me.

"Yeah him," I said. "Well, his cousin, her name's Helen, she knew I'd been there the day before. I stopped by the fish plant in Neil Harbour for directions. I talked with her. Well, she probably told her cousin I'd been there before. Maybe you don't know about small towns. Small towns, well, history happens quicker in small towns." I shrugged in the dark. "By today I was just an old friend dropping by." Then I added, "I don't think they like you much. The Comptons, I mean. Not you personally."

Suzanne's snort of laughter was derisive. "Granddad's influence hasn't penetrated Smelt Brook, I guess. Remind me not to move there."

She might deprecate Smelt Brook's opinion of the Compton family, but for a while she seemed pensive, like someone torn. I knew her well enough to name some of the pieces of her fragmented self: Wild child barefoot on the beach. Sober professor. Arrogant Princess. Was one piece caring? Formless lumps of my own fractured identity recoiled from the possibility. Like a slug curls away from salt. I was afraid.

A deep sigh broke her revery. The princess spoke. She said, "You have to level with me, Brigid. Did you mention Julie?"

"Why should I have?"

"Well, you tell me. Why did you go see Mrs. MacDonald? Pearl is furious with you by the way."

I tried to remember that feeling of bravado that had carried me north and east the night before instead of south and west. I couldn't quite.

"Well?" she rapped.

"Well what? I don't remember why I went." But then, suddenly, I began to remember that grand feeling of brave defiance, that surge of self-confidence when I determined to thwart Pearl, and prove to myself—and to Suzanne—that Brigid Donovan was no push-over. The memory of my euphoria made me forget the rest of it, forget my uneasiness about the light in the barn window, and the sisters' unusual behavior. Forget that I had gone to find Mrs. MacDonald because I was sure that she, at least, would never lie to me. That from her I might get some straight answers.

"My grandfather," said Suzanne abruptly, smashing my cozy feeling of remembered bravery. "He'll want to debrief you when we get back to Halifax."

"Debrief me," I muttered. Hospitably, I hope.

"Yes. Debrief you. I went way out on a limb for you. You don't seem to appreciate that. Grandfather is not happy having our name linked to the MacDonald's. I swore you had the brains God gave you and wouldn't say *anything* until you had a lawyer to talk for you. Grandfather will not be pleased."

He wasn't either, as I found out the next afternoon.

Chapter 12

We had been invited to cocktails before supper. Informal, Suzanne said, unprepared, as it turned out, for what informal meant to me.

"You'll have time," she suggested, "to shop in Halifax. We're not expected until five."

The Andrew Jacksons Pearl had given me were long gone, ditto most of Sister Marie's pretty Canadian bills. I hadn't, of course, stopped in Antigonish to search for a thrift shop, and my clothes had slipped from bad to vile.

"Is there a Sears in Halifax?" I wondered.

"I couldn't say," she said. "Why do you ask?"

This amiable conversation took place over breakfast at an Irving restaurant just west of Antigonish.

"I thought, if there were, I could pick up some trousers and a shirt." I waved my fingers at my pits, delicately.

Suzanne looked astonished, then she laughed. "Good God, Brigid! not that informal."

I stirred my black and sugarless coffee a while thinking about formal and informal. I said, finally, "Then tell me."

"Well, I told Grandfather you hadn't any formal attire with you. And, of course, he understood that."

Seeing she didn't intend to spell it out, I asked, "So what's suitable?"

She looked me over. "I think you could get by with a suit, say a linen suit. And pumps," she added with a pretty pout, acknowl-edgment, I guess, that the pumps were obvious. "Don't worry about jewelry. I'll have something."

"When you say a suit…, " I said.

She looked at me brightly.

"Er, you mean with a skirt?"

"Of course with a skirt!"

I waited to respond until we were in the van. I said I'd drive. Suzanne was reluctant, but she surrendered the keys.

"About this informal dinner," I said. "For me formal is every-thing clean. If I wore a skirt I'd feel like I was in drag. Suzanne, it's not going to happen."

Well, she went on about it till we got to Halifax. I finally said I thought her granddad had her bamboozled and I wasn't too sure I even wanted to meet him. I also told her I was dead broke and couldn't really afford to buy the pants and shirt. I said, "What I really need is a thrift store. But I guess you wouldn't know about that either!"

"Actually, I do," she answered. "My students," she explained.

How we settled it is she asked could she dress me from her wardrobe and I conceded that I'd give it a try. It turned out to be fun, like dress-up. And after a lot of horsing around we settled on something outlandish. "If you can't get it right," Suzanne said, "then go for outlandish." I'd done it before, but never with such panache: Harem style pants, full and many-colored, and a sequined jersey under a see-through blouse. We debated a wig, blonde and cut in a twenties bob. But in the end I declined.

Once she was satisfied with me, Suzanne helped me to undress. It had gotten to be nearly five, and I felt myself rent between two needs. Or between a need and a desire. What I wanted was to frolic on the bed a while. The way Suzanne stripped my finery from me made me think she might want to also.

My need, however, was to make sure she did not offend Old Granddad by showing up late at his cocktail hour. It wasn't my problem, just my co-dependency kicking up. I bent and whispered in her ear, "I think you better scrub my back…this see through blouse and all."

She jumped to her feet, burdened with discarded raiment. In a fussy little voice she said, "Brigid, grow up! I have to iron these. Go bathe, then I will. If we don't leave here in thirty-five minutes, we'll be late."

As it turned out, old man Compton liked my outfit. He seemed to, and afterwards Suzanne confirmed it. "He really thought you looked terrific," she giggled. "Now, if I'd come decked out like that, he'd have cut my allowance."

Cut her allowance. That, I thought, explained a lot.

Old man Compton was charm itself. In his nineties, he chose to sit in a wheelchair, always accompanied by an attendant. "Charles," he introduced him, "my doppelgänger. You'll get used to Charles."

Only Suzanne, the old man and his shadow, and I gathered for drinks. In the solarium. Under a ten foot avocado tree, Mr. Compton quizzed me. As Suzanne had warned, my conduct in Smelt Brook had displeased him.

"Young lady," he said, "you were instructed to wait for a lawyer."

But that was the extent of his chiding. I had a feeling, though, that my conduct was filed for him to use another time should the need arise. I didn't mind. I never intended to see him again. I toyed with calling him on that "young lady," but decided if he dropped my insubordination, I'd let him off the hook. He may have sensed this. If so, our complicity was tacit. But thereafter he referred to me as "Suzanne's friend." And then later, sometime during dinner, he began to say, "my friend, Brigid."

Cocktail hour was just that, an hour. Promptly at seven the old man said, "Charles, we'll retire now." And, smooth as machinery, Charles rolled him out. The old man was right, I had forgotten all about Charles.

"We'll go up to my room," said Suzanne, "until dinner."

"Your room?"

"Oh yes indeed." She laughed. "My apartment in town is not recognized by the family."

The Compton mansion, built of sandstone and not far from

Dalhousie, was massive. A giant cube four stories high, it occupied an entire block. Like the convent of St. Therese, the grounds represented not only money, but time. Lots of time for the massive oaks in front, and lots of money for the flowering shrubs and trees, the masses of daffodils blooming randomly, for myriad flower beds, fountains and, in back, a topiary 'zoo.'

However marvelous the grounds, the house itself was graceless as the Bastille, with scant decoration, just small pediments above windows and two squat columns flanking a monumental front door. Eddie MacDonald had not been the architect.

Inside, the story was different. The entry hall and rooms on either side were as elegant as Versailles. They were rooms of State, marble-floored, gilded, mirrored, and cold. I only caught a glimpse of them. The solarium was in back, through a door behind the graceful sweep of a marble staircase. After drinks, Suzanne and I went up a back stairway to her room. The second floor resembled a hotel, one in Eastern Europe. Not Stalinist, nineteenth century. Biedermeier comfort in the wide hallways and thick carpeting, the glass-fronted bookcases and upholstered sofas placed invitingly under lighted sconces on flocked wallpaper.

Quite opposite the harsh, if aristocratic elegance of below, Suzanne's room was a small apartment, with bath and dressing room. Besides the canopied bed, islands of furniture—a chaise lounge and sofa, each with a flanking table and easy chair—floated on a sea of Persian rugs.

She laughed. "See why I had to get away!"

Her grandfather, she called him 'The Old Man,' had come as a boy to Canada. "After the 1905 revolution. It was Russia then. Poland now. He made good." Her gesture embraced the opulence.

I said, "I guess." I asked about his injury.

"Injury?" Suzanne echoed.

"The wheelchair."

"Oh that," she said. "It's nothing. He just likes Charles handy. And he hates to exercise. He says. I suspect he works out when the rest of us are sleeping".

"Let me tell you," she went on, "who will be at dinner. It's just the family. Eddie MacDonald." She held up one finger. "That's

Pearl's son. The architect."

I nodded.

"You know him?"

"No. Never met him. But his name keeps popping up."

"Doesn't it," she said sourly, and I wondered why. "So, Eddie will be there. The Old Man. And my parents, Paul and Lucy. Just an 'intimate gathering.'" She mouthed the cliche. "My father, this side of the family, we're supposed to be the brainy ones. David, that's Arjuna, he was supposed to be the one who would go on making money."

She had wandered over to a window. Outside, a maple tree shed pale propellers in the sun. Her face turned toward me in profile, the sun backlighting the beauty of her mouth.

I said, " So Arjuna was something of a disappointment."

"Arjuna? No. He wasn't a disappointment. It's this side of the family who disappointed him."

I waited. She turned, picked up a slim volume from the brass table by the chaise and tossed it to me. "Catch!" she said. And I did.

It was a book of poetry, privately printed, the paper luxurious. *Seasons*, by Paul Compton. It was numbered. Five.

"Read one," she said.

I opened the book and read. It wasn't good and it wasn't bad. It was in form, lyric, a little saccharin.

"It was well reviewed," said Suzanne, her tone ironic. "At least in Granddad's paper it was. If you want one, there are several boxes in the attic. You could probably even get a fairly low number. My number is five, after Grandpa, Mother and Arjuna."

"That would be four," I pointed out.

She hit one fist off the other. "Did I forget to mention Pearl?" she asked sardonically.

I wondered at her bitterness toward Pearl and toward Pearl's son, Eddie. Was it envy? Her discontent with her own family's contribution to the Compton demesne was obvious. Her discontent and her frustration. I asked, "He doesn't write any more? Your father."

"Oh, certainly. Every day. Like Trollope. Well, not like

Trollope exactly."

And she laughed, the sound hard and sharp as a cleaver. "Mostly I think it's funny, but sometimes the bathos gets to me. I mistake it for pathos. But they have a good life, Paul and Lucy. For them. I needed to get away. Not that I've gotten very far."

The Old Man, disappointed in the literary achievements of his intellectual son, had cast a different role for his grandson. "'Who never was," said Suzanne. "Well, he was but he died. Crib death. When he was still an infant. So Grandfather had to settle for me."

What he settled on for Suzanne was an academic career, but so far he had been disappointed in that also.

"I've tried," Suzanne said, "but I keep discovering things about myself that aren't on his agenda. Like liking the ladies. That was a biggie. When I got my apartment on Weston Street. But, in general, I have a hard time being serious about.... Oh, *The Adaptability Correlate of Major Religions in the Context of Traditional Cultures and/or Indigenous Populations.*"

She said it rhythmically, like a poem, a bad one. I said I could understand how it could happen, not taking the groves of academe seriously.

"What would you rather do?" I asked.

"It doesn't hardly matter. Right now I'd just like to get tenure at least. Oh, I'm sure I will. Granddad is on Dalhousie's board. And they want a new library. But I do have to get my thesis published. I mean, it can't seem too corrupt!"

"That's enough?" I asked. "Getting tenure?"

"Enough for me? God no. But until I do that, I can forget about the rest."

What the rest was I didn't find out for a while. Just then the chimes for dinner sounded in the hall. "Like on a ship," I said. "At sea."

Chapter 13

Everyone at dinner was charming. The Old Man, honed by age to sharp essentials, dominated the company with grace and playful good humor, slightly mischievous, like a favorite child who takes advantage of his privileges shrewdly, never going too far. He had me sit beside him. Without a prying question, he had from me much of my life's story.

The early unfortunate decision to enter a Religious order right out of high school. My disastrous marriage, and the twins. He even had from me details like Heidi and Alicia.

Heidi, who had been a kind of safety net, briefly breaking my free fall from convent to marriage, from marriage to what became the solitary life of an anchorite. Solitary, that is, except for my little brown jug.

Alicia I had met in a bar somewhere on the lower East Side of Manhattan. We had moved to Maine together, drifted up there after her first encounter with the DTs, enough to sober anyone. Except that it hadn't. Not for a while anyway. We tried a geographic cure instead. But trouble followed us.

Somehow I told the little gnome all of this at dinner, during the passage of many dishes, soup and game, fish and fowl. A medieval feast. Missing only some dogs to lick our fingers clean between courses. Servants brought little finger bowls instead, and warm linen towels.

"That's why," he said thoughtfully, when I told him about the men who brought the jacket with funny long arms for Alicia to wear, "that's why I couldn't tempt you, even with the pick of my cellar." It seemed to make him sad. He held up his glass and examined, in the dazzle of his chandelier, its ruby red contents.

The gesture to his doppelgänger was unobtrusive. Charles' head dipped briefly between us, and then he exited silently to return a moment later with a bottle of French wine which he opened and offered to his master. The old man nodded his approval. Charles filled my empty glass.

I protested. Old man Compton reached over and stopped my mouth with a gentle touch of his finger. "Trust me," he said, "and try it."

I was aware of silence at the table. Everyone busily eating, too courteous to look, but clearly waiting to see what I would do. Even Charles, behind me, for once made his presence felt: he had stopped breathing.

I touched my lips to the surface of the pale pink liquid, the way I do when, rarely, I take communion. The wine, as Julie might say, was awesome. I wanted more.

"Oh come," the old man said. "You don't trust me."

Our eyes met over the rim of my glass. His were amused. "Swallow it," he urged.

I did.

People began again to breath. Conversation resumed. Charles dropped out of my consciousness.

"Well?" he prompted.

"Well, what?" I said. Always gracious.

He laughed. "You are going to learn to trust me," he asserted, wagging a finger at me. "That wine is not alcoholic. You can have as much as you want of it. You see, you are not the first guest who prefers to abstain. And then, at Lent, all of us choose this." He topped up my glass. He winked.

Much as I liked the wine—it was dry and light, not some car-bonated Welch's grape juice—I resented the old man's easy confidence. My resentment forced me to acknowledge something I had been trying to ignore, a certain contempt I harbored for Suzanne. For her subservience to the old man's wishes. I realized now that this patriarch had more going for him than the carrot and stick of his money. He was manipulative, but he was charming, and he was bold. He was hard to resist. Like the rest of the company, I had found myself pretty willing to jump whenever he snapped his fingers—drinking his wine, playing True Confessions.

Later, what seemed most remarkable to me about the evening was how I had recited that second-rate melodrama, aka my life, to him. It was done sporadically, for he maintained throughout a gentle badinage with the others which I too took part in. Amazingly, not once during the hour and a half of dinner—nor afterwards—did I taste that bitter feeling of humiliation, like bile, that comes from vomiting an undigested past.

This, I learned later from Suzanne, was my debriefing. By the time my tale took up the events of the previous afternoon at Smelt Brook, I had forgotten my resentment of the wine episode and was babbling contentedly. Mr. Compton squeezed my hand to reassure me when I explained why I hadn't waited for his lawyer.

"Helen, that's the woman who took me to her home. It was her cousin who questioned me. Helen had been so kind, and there was nothing to hide...."

He had reached into my lap, found my hand and taken hold of it. "Would've done the same myself," he said. "But you know lawyers. Worry, worry, worry. But then, that's what I pay them for!"

"Eddie! How's that Inverness project coming? I understand," the old man said, turning to me and fetching my hand still in his, from my lap to the tabletop, "I understand that you and Suzanne inspected the site. What do you think of that location?"

The company awaited my verdict expectantly. I rewarded them. "Terrific," I said.

Paul, Suzanne's father, chuckled at my wit. And Lucy, his wife, beamed her approval of my repartee. William Powell and Myrna Loy. That would about catch the style, the good looks, and the level of wry sophistication of the 'intellectual' side of the Compton patrimony. Paul looked, I thought, like his poetry, well formed but ineffectual.

Over dessert, old Mr. Compton told me a little about himself. To hear him tell the story, he made his stake by saving money earned selling newspapers when he was just a boy. I let it go. What he did with the money was as interesting to me as where he got it to begin with. Help had come, he told me, from God. Yeah, I thought: You and Sister Barnabas.

"Had to drop out of school, don't you know. Never went past fifth grade," he said with pride. "The Sisters, hear, wanted me to stay, no tuition, but," he shrugged, "times were hard, family had too many other mouths to feed."

God sent help, it seemed, through a young priest. "From the Old Country," said Mr. Compton, meaning Ireland. "Needed help, he did, for the hedge schools. Sure and you know about the hedge schools, an Irish lass like yourself," he said, burlesquing a brogue.

I did, in fact, but as intellectual trivia, not part of my heritage. Before Ireland became independent, it was treason to teach Irish children in their native tongue. Some brave priests did anyway, in the open, 'in the hedges.' Hedge schools. I nodded.

"This was back aways, before '22," the old man continued. "They were still enslaved by the English. So, I gave him my stake. It's a divine law, you know, when you give, God gives back ten-fold. And He did. Ten times ten."

He nodded down the table ladened with silver and gold and the fat of the land.

"Wouldn't you know it, that young priest became head of the new Bank of Ireland under De Valera. Invested my charity in good works there he did.

"Isn't that right, Eddie?"

Eddie, who had been talking across the table to Suzanne, smoothly turned and said, "Absolutely, Grandfather." Then, winking at me, added, "If you say so."

"He's a rascal, that one," declared the old man, his pride in Eddie apparent.

Eddie, forty-some, looked much younger. He resembled the young Arjuna in the picture I had seen in Pearl's hands back at Shangri-La the morning after the fire which had killed him. Arjuna had looked becoming in his turban and bare chest. Eddie was just as becoming in his pin-striped suit and wide silk tie with its jeweled flowers. I realized that the oriental almond eyes I had

96

noticed first in Arjuna, were shared by Eddie and by the old patriarch as well. His had retreated, with age, into their protective sockets, but their shape was the same as the son's and the grandson's. The shape as well as the magnetic eroticism of their fire. I found it hard to pull my eyes away from his.

"Your grandson looks like you," I said awkwardly.

"My grandson? Oh, Eddie. Yes. So I've been told. He's had many advantages," said the old man ambiguously.

He bent forward, his glass held negligently in his hand, the ruby contents dangerously close to the rim, to spilling over onto the unblemished white linen tablecloth. I couldn't see the expression in his eyes, bunkered as they were behind the hard bones of his brow. But he stared at his grandson, Eddie, intently, his shoulders bunched and tense. He reminded me of pictures I'd seen of bird dogs pointing, body strained toward a single object, one paw negligently limp.

Eddie, suave, handsome, at ease, seemed to dominate the far end of the table. He was telling a story. Lucy's face was bright with pleasure; even Paul seemed amused. Not so Suzanne. She rearranged the contents of her plate, busy but uninterested. The expression on her face was close to sullen.

Charles broke the tension, perhaps to save the tablecloth. He whispered from above, "Do you wish more wine, sir?"

I said, "so you made your fortune by investing in hedge schools?" It seemed a safe topic.

The old man, pulled back to the present by two simultaneous demands, started. A drop of wine spilled and spread, ruby red on white.

"You've diversified," I said regretting the tablecloth, regretting his discomfort, wondering at the intensity of his regard for Eddie.

Ignoring the stain, he righted his glass so that Charles could pour. Turning to me he said, "Diversified? Ah, of course. Diversified, yes."

He chucked and sipped his wine. Then he turned, jovial now as before and said, "But all my investments have been faith investments. Isn't that right, Suzanne?"

Suzanne stopped playing with her peas and responded gayly,

"Yes, Grandfather, they have indeed."

No mischief in Suzanne's response. I remembered what she had said about having her allowance cut should she appear at dinner in a get-up like my own. I thought it might pay her to try it on once, she had nothing to lose but her fears. Whatever life roles he had assigned to them, the old man seemed to prefer those offspring who were rascals. I was beginning to understand Suzanne's bitterness. And her frustrations. She must see herself in a no-win situation where Old Man Compton's blueprints for his family were concerned.

"No," I said. "I meant the Buddhist temples. Those investments."

Silence touched the table briefly, like a threat.

"They have nothing to do with me," said the old man coolly.

"But the sign in Inverness. It said the builders were..."

"The Compton Brothers," Eddie interjected, smooth as detergent.

"A different family?" I asked.

"A different stake," the old man said.

I had the feeling that breathing around the table had stopped again. Then Lucy asked something of Eddie in a high little-girl voice and conversation resumed.

"You've met Eddie's mother, I understand." Mr. Compton's voice rustled dryly in my ear. "Pearl MacDonald."

I said, "Yeah. I've got her van."

"That's right. I believe you've been making some deliveries for the poor."

I didn't contest it. Though I no longer believed that that was why Pearl had given me the van and a hundred dollars.

"Suzanne tells me," the old man went on, "that you've met Pearl's sisters. Lovely women. Faith and Hope. You know, her name, Pearl's name, was Charity."

"That's what I understand."

"Terrible tragedy, " he murmured.

He looked suddenly diminished. I wondered which tragedy he had in mind. The death of his son, Arjuna, the murder of old Mrs. MacDonald, or Julie's kidnapping. I felt a sudden pang of sympathy toward him.

"More than one," I said. "Tragedy."

"Do you believe," he asked, "that they're connected?"

"Don't you?"

He didn't answer directly. "Pearl seems to value your ability as a detective."

That might, obliquely, be true, I thought. She had gone to some trouble to get rid of me and to get Suzanne to keep an eye on me. But I didn't say anything, just took another sip of wine. A white gloved hand appeared and filled my glass.

The old man dipped into my lap again to find my hand. He held it. His skin was dry and smooth and somehow comforting. "I'm afraid for Julie," he confessed.

"Do you know where she might be?" I asked.

"Know? Of course I don't know," he said judiciously. "Pearl thinks she must still be in Maine. I think so too." Gently he squeezed my hand. "We hope you will help us find her."

I nodded, not in agreement so much as preoccupied with another thought. "Do you have any ideas about Mrs. MacDonald? Pearl's mother, I mean."

"Ideas," he repeated, his voice mournful. "I met her," he said. "I understand you had spoken with her the day before, er…."

"Yes," I said. Suddenly I remembered her vividly. They must have been of an age, the old man at my side and old Mrs. MacDonald. I remembered, with regret, the Shaker-like simplicity of her manner and her house. Regret that I would never be able to rock by her side again there at land's end. I said, "She was quite a woman."

"Yes. Remarkable. Her sacrifice. And so unnecessary really. She was not unlike her daughter Pearl." He paused. "I believe the major suspect in her death, you know, is yourself." He looked at me expectantly.

I didn't reply. My heart had lodged in my esophagus. "Say what?" I mustered.

"Never you mind." That gentle squeeze again. "Help us find Julie," he cajoled. He seemed to take my silence for assent, for he lifted my hand to his lips. He tapped his wine glass. Each head, smiling, turned expectantly.

"Suzanne," the old man said, "Brigid has agreed to help us find Julie. Could you possibly take a few days from your writing to join her?"

It was only a fleeting impression, but it seemed that for an instant Eddie looked chagrined, Suzanne triumphant. But, quick as bubbles bursting, their expressions became passively acquiescent once more.

"Shall we retire?" The old man returned my hand to me. "Do you play billiards, Brigid? I may call you Brigid. A good Irish name it is."

I declined billiards, and after settling 'the young people' in the game room, the old man had Charles roll him off to bed. I realized with a moment's misgiving that Charles must have heard my confessional life story at dinner. I wondered how many such he had listened to, and marveled at the man's ability to slip out of one's consciousness.

I also wondered about that young boy's investment in a hedge school. The IRA and gun-running sounded more likely to me. And I wondered why Ireland, and why an accent that, while slight and not quite definable, was more brogue than Slavic or Canadian. I wondered who his wife was and when she had died.

Suzanne provided some explanations. We lay under the trailing fire plant in her bow window. It was a little past midnight, and way past my bedtime. After the old man went to bed, we had sneaked out the back way and returned to Weston street.

"Where's your grandmother?" I asked her.

"In Vancouver."

"Vancouver?"

"Turn over," she said. "I like to sleep on my right side." She prodded my shoulder. "Mother's family all lives in British Columbia."

"No. Your Compton grandmother."

We rearranged ourselves. Like spoons. Suzanne said, "Oh, her. She died. Childbirth. I never knew her. Get the light, Brigid."

I got it. I tried to turn to face her, but she said, her tongue hot in my ear, "Aren't you comfortable?"

"Oh, yeah. I forgot. You like to sleep on your right side. Suzanne, was she Irish?"

"Anna Maria Zuccollo? Not hardly. Good night, Brigid. Sleep tight, dear."

Over my shoulder I said, "Then how come Ireland, why that brogue?"

Her answer, when it came, was slurred with sleep, her shaggy breath easing the words into my ear. "Protective coloring," she said. Her tongue seemed intent on eating her words, it followed them deep as it could go. The old man's benediction seemed to have revived her affection for me.

"When they first came," she said, then ate a while. "The family converted...Mother worked at the convent." Nibble, nibble. "Servants all Irish. Granddad says...protective coloring...chameleon."

Old man Compton, I reflected, had certainly used his church connections to advantage. Or, as he would have said, "accepted God's help as it came along." Trying to get sleepy, I thought about his being a shirt-tail relative of the Wojtyla family back in Poland. I was pretty sure there had never been a Zuccollo pope. Had Suzanne said 'converted?' Converted from what? If the family had been Jewish, no papal connection there. Perhaps the family had belonged to the Orthodox Church and converted from that. And perhaps I didn't care.

Chapter 14

We rolled into Shangri-La mid-afternoon. The site of the cabin where Arjuna and Julie had stayed—and Arjuna had died—had been cleared of rubble and planted.

"Herbs," Pearl explained, in a brisk, matter-of-fact voice. "Arjuna loved them. I've ordered some rare varieties from Tibet. I hope they do well in this climate. For now we've done what we could, hyssop, savory, rosemary. Rue. And Eddie is making plans for a structure. Something simple. Open. To sit in, you know. Meditate."

She looked at me oddly when I murmured, "A memorial for his father," and I wished I hadn't said it.

"I have to attend a meeting in twenty minutes at H.O.P.E.. Ford Foundation or I would cancel it," she apologized. "But I've arranged for us to have supper together—you, Suzanne and I. I've heard from Julie." Trouble compressed her brow like a vise. "Well, not Julie exactly. Arthur." She waved away my questions. "Not now," she said. "At supper."

I had left Suzanne examining the newly planted herbs while I walked Pearl to her truck. I decided it was as good a time as any to check in with Sister Pat.

I found her baking bread.

"I heard from Pearl you were coming back," she said. "It's going to be dill bread. Fresh from the garden. The dill, I mean."

She was dressed in clean jeans and flannel shirt, despite the heat. I laughed to myself, thinking clean like that she must be going some place formal.

"Your bed's ready," she said. "Upstairs. The milking shed is boarded and roofed. I thought I could get to tar papering tomorrow."

She fiddled with the cookstove, closed the damper a little. "We'll have tea and fresh bread," she said, "in forty-five minutes."

I said, "Wow." She looked pleased, her eyes bright and blue. Then I said, "I have to be back at Shangri-La," and I saw clouds gather around her irises. "Uh, Pearl has heard from Arthur. About Julie."

"That can wait," said Pat. Overriding my protest, she pointed out, "If it was urgent, you'd be talking with her now." She smiled knowingly, "Right?"

"Pearl is meeting with some Ford Foundation people," I said.

"And you're meeting with me. Barney thinks we can sell this dill bread. Pay for the milking shed. She wanted you to test it first. Tell Pearl that you had to help some nuns with market research. That's something Pearl would understand."

Well, I stayed for the bread, and was glad I had. It was terrific. Pat and I hammered some tarpaper in place while we waited for it to bake. When I told her I intended to stay at Shangri-La for the night, she folded her arms across her chest like she thought maybe she had her habit on and not just some jeans and a flannel shirt that weren't even clean any more.

If Pat had said something like, "Love of my life, I can't bear the thought of you being in that woman's arms tonight," who knows, I might have stayed. It wouldn't have been the first time I'd taken a vow of celibacy because of some crazy infatuation with a nun. Of course, the first time I was seventeen. At fifty-five, I might know better; but as futures go, it didn't seem so bad, sleeping next to Pat with just that rough pine boarding between us at night, and fresh dill bread with newly churned butter for breakfast.

But, glowering like a convent school Mother Superior, what Pat chose to say was, "Brigid Donovan! I can't believe you're letting yourself be used by those people."

Her bandanna had slipped, exposing an ear and a mass of orange-red hair hot as her temper. Hot as mine. Frustration spurred us both.

Maybe if I had said, "Pat dearest, fly away from all of this with me," we could have patched things up. But my resentment of churchly authority ran too deep. Beyond reason or my own best interests, I said sarcastically, "Right! Anyone should prefer to be used by Sister Barnabas."

I had named my enemy. It was Pat's turn. "Well, I hope you and that Compton woman enjoy your breakfast tomorrow morning!" she said, but she didn't mean it. She left me standing there, feeling foolish. And mad.

Suzanne was pissed at me too.

"Where did you disappear to?" She met me at the door of Shangri-La's administration building, under Eddie MacDonald's pretty Greek tympanum. She reminded me of a tea kettle on the boil, one arm akimbo, the other pointing my way. "Pearl called, wanted to know when to order dinner. What could I tell her? Where did you go?"

"I was helping some nuns do market research," I said.

"Get serious."

Pearl arrived a few minutes later with a pizza from The Duke of Dough in Bucksport. "They deliver," she explained, "and it seemed less of a hassle. Where were you?" she asked me.

"I was helping some nuns do market research," I explained again.

"How is Pat?" she asked.

"The dill bread was terrific," I temporized.

Suzanne took it in with one eyebrow raised.

Pearl had someone in the kitchen make us a salad, and we settled at the table in her quarters, a large studio apartment pleasantly but not luxuriously furnished. Bowls of tulips and lilac brightened and scented the room. It hadn't the Shaker-like austerity of her mother's little house, but clearly Pearl MacDonald's personal tastes did not run to opulence on the Compton scale.

Pearl's latest word from Jesus/Arthur was once again cryptic, and frightening in part because the meaning was so obscure.

"'Every unhappy family is unhappy in its own way like every faith-less woman is faithless in her own way.'"

"That's it?" I said. "No ransom demand?"

"Just that first time," said Pearl.

"Did you get the money?" I asked.

Pearl nodded at Suzanne, who said, "I have it with me."

It startled me to hear we had been running around Maine and Nova Scotia with $1,000,000 in the van with us. Stupidly I asked, "U.S. or Canadian?" After all, if it was Canadian, it was only worth about $700,000—U.S.

Together they said, absently, "U.S., I think."

What, after all, is $300,000 among friends.

"I think it's odd," I said, "that he hasn't told you where to leave the money. It's been—"

"Two days," said Pearl promptly.

It seemed longer somehow. Old Mrs. MacDonald's murder seemed to have lengthened time for me. I asked, "You don't think, do you, that Arthur had anything to do with killing Mrs. MacDonald? Your mother," I added, realizing suddenly that Pearl had lost both her mother and her granddaughter within the last two days. Plus Arjuna, father of her only child, and someone whom she had cared for deeply, even if she might have regarded their union as rape.

But you wouldn't have known it looking at her, or listening to her. "I called an old friend of yours, Ed Kelly," she said coolly.

Ed Kelly, the old reprobate, former drinking buddy. Former lover, to hear him tell it. Who knows. "Yeah," I said. Invitingly I hoped.

She pursed her lips, puckered them, perhaps her next words tasted sour. "He said to tell you that your bottle of Jamison's is growing mold. And he sends his love. He told me that it's not unusual for kidnappers to soften up their victims by sending pointless but frightening notes for a few days before giving instructions where to leave the money."

"Oh." I thought about the ransom notes and how oddly eclectic they were. "The first quote," I said, "obviously is from the Bible. And you know, I think the second one is from Othello.

Othello says that line—about rather being a toad than sharing her—right before he strangles Desdemona. If we had a Bartlett's we could check it out."

"And this latest quote?" Pearl asked the question as much of Suzanne as of me. Suzanne the family scholar, I remembered.

I asked Suzanne, "Do you agree with me about Othello?"

"I don't know Othello," she said. "But it fits. Pearl's told me he was obsessed with Julie. And he was jealous of Arjuna."

"Do you think Arthur killed Arjuna?"

"Yes. Don't you?" they asked.

Suzanne and Pearl began to argue about where the search for Julie and Arthur/Jesus should begin. They seemed to have forgotten the presence of that master sleuth, Brigid Donovan, in their very midst.

Suzanne asked what the police were doing. Pearl told her they had been checking motels and abandoned buildings, flying over woods and offshore islands in helicopters, and they were checking all the border crossings into Canada.

"They can forget abandoned buildings and off-shore islands," said Suzanne.

"Why?" I asked.

They both seemed startled at my question. Maybe they really had forgotten I was there. Or maybe there was a rule I didn't know about. Like when hirelings are to be seen and when they can be heard as well.

"Why?" Suzanne echoed. Then she patiently explained, "Julie wouldn't hear of it."

"Who's the kidnapper?" I asked.

They looked at me impatiently. Then Pearl said, "You mean that Arthur will be calling the shots."

"Well, if it's a kidnapping, that seems likely."

Pearl chewed the fleshy end of her thumb a while before she said, "You're right, of course. But I agree with Suzanne. It's hard to imagine Arthur telling Julie what to do."

"Maybe," I agreed. "But, presumably, he's snapped. I mean," I amended, "even worse than before. What I think is, we need to know a whole lot more about him. Like, where'd he come from? I bet there's a record on him at BMHI." Bangor Mental Health Institute.

Pearl brought out a cardboard box about six inches deep. "This is everything of his I could find," she said setting it on the table. We pawed through the contents. There was a notebook with some aphorisms and Biblical quotes and sketches of a woman who might have been Julie. A tiny edition of the gospels, on tissue thin paper, carried a Lewiston address on the inside cover.

"That's a shelter," said Pearl. "The Good Samaritan. Now I think about it, that is where he came from. Lewiston. Why don't the two of you go there and see what you can discover. I'll check out BMHI. Brigid has a point," she said to Suzanne. "However much Arthur was under Julie's thumb, obviously something else is going on now. We should find out what we can about him."

I said I thought the police were probably already looking into Arthur. But we all agreed that if they were, it was information they had not seen fit to tell Pearl. Though it was nearly eight and already dusk, Suzanne and I decided to hit the road.

"Not to worry," said Suzanne. "I'll drive. You can sleep. We'll be there by eleven."

I hankered to call Sister Pat and tell her how innocent my night looked to be, and how uninteresting my breakfast tomorrow.

As it turned out I didn't sleep much on that trip to Lewiston. Suzanne wanted to know more about "this nun you've been seeing." I told her there wasn't much to tell, which, sadly, was true.

"I wouldn't let that bother me, you know," said Suzanne confidingly. "Her being a nun." We were at the Belfast by-pass. "You want to stop at McDonald's?" she asked.

"What for?"

"You name it. Coffee? Pit stop?"

"Both," I decided.

The place was full of teenagers, so we got our coffee and split. Back in the car, I couldn't remember what we'd been saying, just had this nagging sense there was something I wanted Suzanne to explain.

"You were saying," I tried.

She didn't need prompting. "In my experience, which is not trivial—I spent decades in convent schools—nuns don't need a whole lot of coaxing. But then you should know."

Irrationally, I bridled at her observation, not because it was necessarily untrue, but because she had included Pat in the common herd. I bit my lips to keep from saying, huffily, "Pat's different." Instead, truculently, I said, "Brilliant! And what about Sister Barnabas, her partner in Christ?"

"Her!" Suzanne exclaimed with contempt. "Don't let Barney stop you. I hear she's got other irons in the fire anyway."

This conversation had a *deja vu* quality. I'd heard this song before and not too long ago. From an old friend and erstwhile lover, Georgie Hendryks. Georgie's advice was one reason I'd begun to spend so much time at the Cloisters. But Pat seemed to take my interest as a desire to resume my vows. I sighed.

"Trust me on this one," said Suzanne.

"Suzanne, compared to me, Holden Caulfield is smooth."

I took her silence for agreement.

In a while, grumpily, I asked, "What's this about Barney's other irons?"

"Some nun. Or ex-nun. Lives down around Surry, on some island. She heals. Or so they say. I forget her name. Saint someone or other."

"Santa Clara," I said gloomily. Recalling my sad experience of her. Once upon a time she had been a nun. She led a voluntary community not far from Surry. Called Monte Cassino, it too was situated on a semi-island connected to the mainland at low tide. Santa Clara of the magnetic eyes bedded practically everyone, though I somehow had not been able to keep my place in line. The thought of her and Barney disgusted me. "No way," I said. "Not Barney."

"Right, chief!" said Suzanne. "My, you do get around!"

I ignored her sally.

"They have a business arrangement," she said.

"You mean monkey business?"

"That, too, maybe. No, Pearl says they intend to set up another sideshow there in Soperton. To compete with Julie's stigmata."

Santa Clara had been attracting attention for her putative healing powers for a long time. If Barney was getting in on the act, it meant photographs on coffee cups and autographed T-shirts. Suzanne seemed to relish the idea. It crossed my mind that she might relish even more the possibility that Sister Barnabas and Santa Clara would drive Julie out of business. Pearl, too, for that matter. I realized that the Compton clan was ruled by jealousy as much as anything. Old man Compton's arsenal of manipulation included not just charm and power, but divide and conquer tactics as well.

After a pause, Suzanne added, sounding slightly dejected, "Of course, Pearl hopes to join forces with Barney and Clara. She has a way of doing that with opposition. She joins it. How come she has so much influence with the Old Man, I guess."

I stayed awake clear to Lewiston mulling over all the implications of what Suzanne had told me. It explained a lot.

Knowing how shifty Barney is, I believed it would be like her to befriend Julie before hatching a plot to put her out of business. Long ago Barney had even been sweet to me. Then she tried to blackmail me and I told her to take a hike.

It convinced me, too, that Barney had been less concerned with Julie's safety when she set me up to investigate Pearl than she was to gather dirt wherever there might be some—in Pearl's backyard or Arjuna's. If Pearl were only half as bright as she seemed to be, she would want to be on top of any investigation of herself that Sister Barnabas instigated. And she would go about that by paying for it. That was the Compton style.

But what really kept me awake was this warm tremor of excitement, like a singing telephone wire vibrating inside me. Barney had been buzzing around Santa Clara for years now trying to make honey. If she succeeded and went to live with her, maybe Pat and I could live alone together at the Cloisters. Yeah!

Chapter 15

It was half past eleven when we hit the Lewiston turn-off. We decided to check into a motel and take up our sleuthing in the a.m. Like cousins we were all night, albeit kissing ones.

The Good Samaritan was located down on Water street in an abandoned warehouse by the river. A Bates College student doing an internship greeted us. Her name was Connie.

"How may I help?" she chirped. Like the nuns up around Surry, she wore jeans, a flannel shirt and a bandanna. Unlike theirs, hers were designer jeans, and the shirt was from L. L. Bean. The bandanna, though, was Zayre's. Her bright youthfulness contrasted sharply with the dingy interior of the reception hall.

Suzanne took over. "We've lost someone," she said.

Connie nodded sympathetically. "It happens," she smiled, warm and understanding.

The two of them were broadcasting on the same wave length. The call letters were CLASS.

"His name is Arthur," explained Suzanne. "Though he prefers to be called Jesus."

Connie's face lost some of its luster. "Poor Arthur," she said. "Everyone is looking for him. And that woman, what's her name...?"

"Julie MacDonald," I said.

Connie seemed surprised to see me there. "Yes," she said to

Suzanne. "Julie MacDonald. Poor woman. Are you...?"

Suzanne, funereal as a camel, nodded and said, "She's my niece."

Connie commiserated in appropriately soft tones before saying, "The police, of course, checked here. I don't see any reason not to tell you what I told them. Which isn't much."

The not much was an address in Harlem. I recognized it. The Emmaus Hotel. I'd been there before on another case, a missing novice from Pat's convent. I nudged Suzanne in the side. "I know that place," I said.

"If you like," said Connie, ignoring me, "I could call them for you."

It occurred to me there was more than class tying these two together. I wanted to say, "She doesn't eat breakfast," but restrained myself.

Suzanne, by this time a dazzling smile on legs, said, "Thank you, Connie, but that won't be necessary." Then she said, "I'm sorry it was a tragedy that brought me here. I'd like to come back and find out more about this shelter sometime. Maybe you could show me around."

"Yeah," I said, taking Suzanne's arm. "She'll want to know more about the adaptability correlate among indigenous populations to your store-front Christianity." My eye had caught a tattered calendar nailed to the wall above the desk. Jesus looked apologetic about the blood from his heart dripping all over his hand. Something had gnawed away one corner. Thrusting my chin at the sorry-looking calendar, I said, "'Indigenous' in this case must mean rats. Let's go!"

Suzanne was amused. So was Connie. Big deal.

We left Lewiston for the Big Apple about eight-thirty, and rolled into Harlem a little after one. Suzanne drove. I like to keep closer to the speed limit. She took 95 the whole way. I always go Sawmill to Henry Hudson. No trucks. I wondered, gloomy when I wasn't terrified, whether our preference for different routes was a visible sign not of Grace but of a generation gap. I remembered sentimentally when Pat and I had made the trip together a few years before.

We managed to park directly in front of Emmaus. I said I'd handle things.

A line of people stood waiting at the door. "They serve lunch, a soup kitchen," I explained to Suzanne. We by-passed the line and went on in. Security, a tall dude with two earrings—both in the same ear—asked us our business.

"Is Father X in?" I asked.

"Nope. He in Maine."

"That's where we just came from," I said.

He shrugged. "Too bad."

Suzanne took over. "We're trying to locate someone who used to live here."

"I know, don't tell me," he said. "You want the address of Jesus' next a kin." He pronounced it Spanish, hay-soos. "You from Maine, how I knew," he grinned.

"Police been here asking?" said Suzanne.

"Yeah, and a lady, she call from Maine. A place call Surly. Ain't that a name."

"Surry," I corrected.

"With a fringe on top? Oklahoma, right?"

Our friend was high on something, Jesus maybe. The one with the bleeding heart.

"Do you have the address?" Suzanne prompted.

"You hold on a minute, this crowd get settle. I get the address for you."

On Jose's suggestion—we had exchanged names—we joined the line for lunch. Chicken soup, croissant sandwiches, sourdough French bread, and salad. Suzanne was amazed. "Left-overs," I explained. "From the best hotels."

"I guess."

The dining hall held about a hundred people, mostly men. All hungry. Like Suzanne and me.

Jose joined us for coffee. The address he gave Suzanne was in the Village. "That some dude, that Jesus," Jose observed.

"What do you mean?" I asked.

"He really think he be Jesus!"

This time Jose said it American, with a "g."

"Father X, now, he don't like that one bit. Cause I tell you, Father X, he think he be Jesus." Jose laughed, and then he laughed some more. He was still laughing and wiping his eyes as Suzanne and I thanked him and made our way out.

Downtown our luck turned sour. Denise Lafferty was the name. The address, on Hudson Street. According to Jose, Denise Lafferty was Arthur's mother. "Aka, Maria," Jose had said. "Get it? Jesus? Maria?"

Suzanne had said yes, she got it.

On Thirteenth Street, she parked the van, and we started downtown on foot. There had been a shower earlier, and the soft spring air was as fresh as it gets in Manhattan. It made me cheerful. It seemed to make most everyone cheerful—Suzanne, young mothers with strollers loaded with babies; even taxicab drivers seemed more cheerful than usual. But a scan of the names on the mailboxes at the address Jose had given us, brought gloom. No Lafferty, no Denise. Suzanne rang a bell at random.

The buzzer sounded. We entered a narrow hallway with stairs on our left, a door to the right. Stretching past the stairs the hall continued, even more narrow and dimly lit. A third door could be seen in the gloom.

"Let's try that one," said Suzanne. "It looks mysterious."

Just then the door opened. My heart did a two-step around in my chest. It was Sister Pat!

Of course it wasn't. But they could have been sisters, the blood kind. This woman's hair was also brightly hennaed. But she wore an outfit Pat wouldn't have been caught dead in, more like something you'd find hanging in Suzanne's closet.

"Can I help you?" the woman asked, her voice flutey with an odd accent, not quite British, not quite anything I had ever heard before.

Suzanne and I moved down the hall. It had a sweet-sour smell of disappointment that matched the melancholy grime of the walls, the hopeless light cast by a twenty-watt bulb.

"Yes?" the woman asked as we drew close.

"We're looking for Denise Lafferty," I said, fascinated by her resemblance to Pat, even up close.

"Well, you got the wrong apartment." She started to shut the door.

"Please," I said. "Hold on. We're trying to find her son. It's urgent."

She relented enough to keep the door open a crack. Through it she said, "Try St. Elizabeth's."

"St. Elizabeth's?"

"The hospital!"

She slammed the door. The noise, reverberating between the narrow walls, momentarily relieved the settled gloom: Action! Change! Armageddon maybe.

Outside in the new spring air, Suzanne exclaimed, "Is she on drugs or what! "

"What," I said, remembering my own Big City Blues, my own slammed doors, some due to my buddy, Bottle, but not always.

Suzanne and I parted at the parking lot. The family, she said, kept a pied-a-terre on Central Park West. Three Hundred, Central Park West. We arranged to meet there. She trusted me, she said, to investigate St. Elizabeth's on my own. Besides, she was tired.

"We can call for Chinese take-out when we get hungry. Or," she added, "you could pick something up on your way. There's a grocery on Amsterdam."

I knew the grocery, I knew the address. The grocery was not on the way. I let it go. Chinese sounded good to me.

"Anyway," said Suzanne, climbing into the van, "we'll need coffee and milk. Bread too. And butter."

As she started off I yelled after her, "Call and have them deliver."

The Mouse that Roared!

It took just over two hours to pry the information about Denise Lafferty out of St. Elizabeth's. Three items: She had died there. Her profession was architect. The name listed to notify was Heidi McCarren. 348 -1212.

That wasn't the number I called. By the time I got it, it was nearly six o'clock. Heidi's office would be closed. She herself would be stuck somewhere in traffic. Homeward bound. No problem, I had her home number in my little black book in the side pocket of my knapsack.

Heidi McCarren was my Heidi. Other mother to the twins. Although sometimes it had seemed to me that it was I, not she, who was their other mother. Heidi got sober before me. I thought at the time it was just another way she had to be a pain in the ass.

I didn't have a number for Suzanne. I hoped she didn't get too hungry waiting for me to arrive with viands. I didn't think she would. I examined the crumpled bills in my pocket. A ten and six ones. Plenty for a cheeseburger and a subway token. Life was good.

The cheeseburger wasn't. But, I had money enough left to get some cherry flavored Rolaids. Like an after-dinner mint. A geriatric after-dinner mint. Then I called Heidi.

She said what she could tell me about Denise Lafferty she didn't want to tell me over the phone, not after a hard day at the office. Heidi owned a small architectural firm where she combined a fine business acumen with a flair for designing spaces fitted to the needs of woman and children. She suggested I mosey uptown and have dinner with her.

"Pick up something on the way," she said. "I'm all out of everything."

"Yeah," I said. "Right."

Some things there's no point in fighting.

Why do I always get involved with people who mistake me for a gofer? Heidi and Suzanne, they'd used the exact same words: Pick up something on your way. On my way? Give me a break.

I ordered sweet and sour pork. Yeah, sweet and sour. Heidi hates it. I couldn't help myself. While I waited, I went to the Korean grocery store two doors down for a cantaloupe.

"What did you get?" asked Heidi, after she had greeted me with a hug and some kisses.

"Sweet and sour pork."

"You're kidding."

"And a cantaloupe."

She opened the carton. "You're not kidding. Did you get something for yourself?"

What she meant was, did I have something else she might like better.

I didn't tell her I had exactly seven cents in my pocket. I said I had already eaten. Which was true enough.

It was no Shui-hu Rou, but Heidi gobbled up the sweet and sour as if she liked it. We shared the cantaloupe. And she told me about Denise Lafferty.

It was, Heidi said, a sad story. She looked at me reproachfully. Her look said, "You're my sad story." I may have been one of them. Left her for another woman. Or so it seemed. What I left her for was the bottle. Alicia came afterwards, almost incidentally.

Heidi and Denise Lafferty had been students together at Pratt. Heidi, who had worked as a draftsman in dead-end jobs for years, had decided to go back to school to get her degree and become licensed. She had fallen in with a group of younger students, attracted, she said, to Denise.

"That wasn't on," said Heidi. The memory still seemed to rankle. We sat in her living room, high on the twentieth floor, the lights of the city bright around us, brighter than the pale light of candles in the branched candelabra before us. The eye of a sandalwood joss stick glowed red in the gloom.

"Why?" I threw into the deepening silence. "Why wasn't it on?"

"She was in love. Some pretty boy. Canadian. Rich. A real jerk."

Her disappointment shaded her judgement. Rich, Canadian, pretty. Maybe even a jerk. But a man, nonetheless, of some substance, material substance as well as substance of character. I knew, had known with an eerie presentiment, or so it seemed there in the wavering light of the candles, that Denise Lafferty's story would loop back to the Comptons.

"What was his name?" I asked.

"Eddie. Eddie MacDonald," she said.

116

Chapter 16

"What happened?" I asked.

Heidi didn't answer for a while, reflecting, I imagined, as much on what hadn't happened as on what had. She wore a Chinese robe, a lustrous silk brocade of blue so deep it seemed to dissolve in the darkness of the room. But writhing in its spilling folds, the metallic coils of a dragon shimmered occasionally like something alive at her feet.

"The usual. She got pregnant," Heidi said at last. She sighed.

"Did he marry her?" I asked.

"Finally. Finally he did. Right before the baby was born. A little girl, Julia."

The marriage had been a civil ceremony down at City Hall. Heidi hadn't attended. Hadn't been invited.

"That was fine with me," she said. At her feet, the dragon's jaw snapped shut, its tail lashed. "If it hadn't been for me, though, there wouldn't have been a wedding. Maybe I shouldn't have interfered."

Maybe that was true, but Heidi's middle name was Interference. I waited for her to go on.

"Well, they were neither of them Flower Children—this was sixty-six. Well before Woodstock. But Eddie said he wasn't into marriage. What it was, he was afraid of his dad, afraid he'd be disowned."

"Grandfather," I corrected.

"No his father. So I wrote to him."

There was a momentary frenzy at her feet, then the dragon fell somnolent again.

"You wrote to Arjuna? David Compton?"

"Who's Arjuna?"

"Eddie's father." I started to explain the family tree to her. "See, Jacob Compton is the patriarch of the family. An immigrant, just a boy when his family came to Halifax. Nineteen six they got here. Got there."

"Is he still alive."

"Oh yeah. Alive and rich. He had two sons."

"Eddie and who else."

"No, not Eddie. Now, you let me tell this part of the story," I chided.

"Well, it was Jacob Compton I wrote to," Heidi asserted. "I remember now. I wondered at the difference in the names."

"Well, I'm sure that you did write to Jacob. He runs things. But he's Eddie's grandfather. Eddie's father, David, got involved with a young woman, a servant, from the St. Therese orphanage. Her name is Pearl MacDonald. The old man, Jacob, is a big patron of St. Therese. What surprises me is that the old man made Eddie marry your friend Denise. He certainly didn't make David marry Pearl, although he took care of Eddie's education as if he were his own son."

"Well," said Heidi "I understood that Jacob was Eddie's father. That's still what I think, but let's not pursue it. It's beside the point."

I had to bite my lips, but we didn't pursue it.

"I wrote to Eddie's father about Denise and the baby. I never heard back, but next thing I knew they were married, and a few weeks later Julia was born. Denise dropped out of school, and we lost touch. Then about five years ago, she applied for a job with me. She'd never gotten her degree, but she was a good draftsman, and I hired her."

The marriage, as might have been foreseen, was not a success, which is why Heidi had mused that maybe she shouldn't have interfered. When Eddie left he took the baby with him. Heidi explained, "Eddie's father, Jacob, made him take the baby. No baby, no inheritance. Jacob wanted his grandchild."

I managed not to say, "His great-grandchild." Since we'd agreed not to pursue this point.

Denise had been devastated. And, she discovered shortly, she was pregnant again.

"With Arthur," I put in.

"Arthur. Right. I guess she'd learned her lesson, so she never even told Eddie about the new baby. She filed for divorce and later married this Lafferty. I guess Arthur was always a little weird. But so was Lafferty. He was a poet, supposedly. Denise supported them. Arthur, Lafferty, and Lafferty's drugs."

I wondered about Denise. Two losers in a row suggested she had some problems of her own. I asked Heidi, "Denise was Miss Rheingold?"

"She drank if that's what you mean. I got her to go to Al Anon. She eventually graduated to AA."

Arthur, perhaps, suffered from fetal alcohol syndrome. Julie, perhaps, did too. Maybe those exotic eyes had their origins in pathology as much as in genes.

For a while neither of us spoke. Heidi sighed some, and the dragon squirmed. Then Heidi continued, "Right before Denise came to work for me Lafferty died. AIDS. I insisted Denise get a blood test, and she tested HIV positive."

"Is that what killed her?"

"Yes. Though they refused right up to the end to admit it. Only faggots get AIDS, you know. What the rest of us get are a lot of unrelated rare diseases."

Heidi fell silent. I knew without asking that she had supported Denise through what must have been a few horrible years. And costly. I regretted my irritation over the issue of Eddie's relationship to old Jacob Compton. "You supported her then," I said softly.

The dragon stirred at her feet. "Someone had to," she said dismissively.

"What happened to Arthur?"

"Arthur/Jesus?" She snorted . "In and out of Bellevue. In and out of the City. When Denise was getting close to the end I wrote to Jacob Compton again. Explained about Arthur. Sent a copy of his birth certificate. Never heard back. But Arthur never showed up again. Haven't seen him for well over a year now."

I wondered which family member had been tapped to locate Arthur and deliver him to Shangri-La. Deliver him to the care of his grandparents, Pearl MacDonald and the rascally monk, Arjuna. I thought probably Suzanne had been the one, she seemed to be everyone's errand girl. Whatever, one thing was clear. The Compton crew knew all they needed to know about Arthur/Jesus. Sending me to New York to find out more about him had been arranged just to get me out of the way.

I puzzled over it a while in silence.

Suzanne must have been confident that I would draw a blank at St. Elizabeth's. Otherwise she would never have left me alone.

Or: Suzanne knew that I would discover the connection to Heidi. She had left me alone so that Heidi and I could talk frankly.

I didn't consider the possibility that Suzanne knew Heidi and I had once been lovers.

Another possibility I didn't consider was that I had been set up. Not me. Not that redoubtable sleuth Brigid Donovan, the detective everybody was so eager to hire.

It hadn't been hard to get Heidi's address. That suggested that Suzanne wanted me to discover that Arthur was Eddie's son. That Arthur and Julia were brother and sister. But why would Suzanne want me to find out? What game was she playing? I could ask her.

Instead, diffidently, I asked Heidi, "Could you lend me some money?"

She laughed. The dragon thought I was funny too. After a while they both settled down.

"Forget it," I said.

She said she was sorry. She asked how much I wanted. Then she asked me what I wanted it for, and when I would repay her.

I decided to work backwards on her questions. "I don't know when I can pay you. What I want it for is to fly to Maine. Tonight if I can. I think two hundred would do it, oh, two-fifty."

"That's why?"

So, I poured out the whole story. When I was done, Heidi said, "The tale of two cities." Even in the dark she must have sensed that I looked at her stupidly.

Impatiently she said, "Not Dickens! St. Augustine."

The Heavenly and the Earthly cities then. But she was wrong and I hastened to set her straight.

"I don't think that the religiosity of the Comptons means much. Let me tell you how that Pearl milks big foundations—"

Heidi cut me short. "I don't mean the Comptons! Of course that religion business of theirs is just that: Business. They're the material part of the equation. Mrs. MacDonald, Pearl's mother, she's the genuine article spiritually. It's too bad the way the Compton's got hold of Pearl after her mother went to prison. Pearl might have been better off serving time for killing that brute, her father. At least she wouldn't have been corrupted by the Comptons."

I thought about it until Heidi broke my reverie. "Take three hundred," she said. "You might need it. The Comptons will never pay you, not for finding out the truth. So don't worry about it. It will be my memorial for Denise. To find her kids."

While I called the airlines, Heidi went "to look for something." She came back to the living room, turning on lights, with a Bartletts in her hand. "Lets find those quotes," she said.

As I thought, the one was from Othello. The other, about the unhappy family and the faithless woman, Heidi found right off. "Family, family, family. Here it is. Unhappy. Seven three two bee. Hmmm. Anna Karenina. Of course, I should have thought of that. 'Happy families are all alike; every unhappy family is unhappy in its own way.' He made up the part about the faithless woman."

She laid the book on the floor by her feet. "It sounds like he had fun finding those quotes," she observed. "He never struck me as having a sense of humor. I guess I underestimated him."

"Who ?"

"Arthur. Isn't that who we've been talking about? You told me Arthur kidnapped Julie. Isn't that right?"

"Yeah," I said, "that's what I told you." But my little gray cells were busy computing something different. I kept silent while they worked.

"Talk to me," said Heidi.

"Wait," I replied, "it's too bizarre." Then, as the new picture began to take form in my mind, I said, "It's crazy!"

"What is bizarre? What's crazy?" said Heidi irritably.

"Arjuna wrote those notes," I declared, though I couldn't have explained how or why.

"Who's Arjuna?"

"Eddie's father. I tried to tell you." I began, excitedly, to explain it over again. "Arjuna and Julia lived together. They cooked up the stigmata for Julie. See, Arjuna, aka David Compton, was something of a rascal, but very lovable I guess. And as a Buddhist monk, as Arjuna, he was very popular with the New Age crowd. Made a lot of money, I guess.

"I told you, Arjuna was murdered. About a week ago. Burned to death. So he couldn't have written these notes. But they are so like him. There's a playfulness to them that never made sense coming from Arthur. But it's crazy. Arjuna's dead. He was dead before the kidnapping, before the notes even started."

I subsided in embarrassment.

Heidi looked at me curiously "Don't be embarrassed," she said.

"Who's embarrassed?"

"You are. You have no self esteem. That's always been your problem. You're afraid of success. That's why you never finished your Ph.D. That's why you buried yourself in Maine. That's—"

"Heidi," I interrupted. "Chill out."

"Right," she acceded, surprising me. We must both be getting old I thought.

"I'm sorry," she said. "But if you think this Arjuna wrote those notes, then he did."

"That's crazy."

"So, what's wrong with crazy. Trust your craziness. That's the issue. Trust. People are so afraid of reality they don't trust it, so they go by appearances instead. You don't. Usually."

"Usually?" I asked.

"Jacob Compton is Eddie's father."

After my reflexive annoyance, I considered it. I found that I liked it. Pearl had been raped by the old man, not by young David, his son. So, old Jacob Compton had *three* sons: Paul, the poet manque; David, the rascally monk, aka Arjuna; and a third—Eddie MacDonald, a bright young man who was a success both as an architect and as a businessman. The Compton Brothers of the construction company were Eddie and David/Arjuna. I understood vaguely why my questions had caused consternation at the dinner party. "A different stake," Jacob Compton had said. He might have said, "A different brother." It had been that rascally monk Arjuna, I imagined, who had exposed the relationship the old man had been at pains to hide.

I thought about the progeny of these three men, that new generation of heirs to the vast Compton fortune. To the fortune and also to the wily machinations that had built the fortune. They were three: Suzanne, Julie and Arthur. Thinking about them made me uneasy.

It didn't take a genius to see that the Comptons were in serious trouble. Out of control. The syllables became a beat in my brain: out-of-control. A long, two shorts, and a long. Two of them plus another long, and you had my buzzer signal in the dorm at St. Andrews. "Out of control, Out of control, Out." Like the old Dragnet theme, "Dum de Dum Dum, Dum de Dum Dum, Dum."

Two murders and a kidnapping. The murders at least were real. The reality of Mrs. MacDonald's corpse—the blood, the flies, the unseeing eyes—was vivid in my mind.

Those two families, the MacDonalds and the Comptons, bound together by fate. A malicious fate, I thought. To Heidi they represented the Heavenly City and the Earthly City, a Manichean contrast between good and evil. Maybe Heidi was right.

I began to worry about the MacDonald sisters in Nova Scotia, Faith and Hope, caught between those forces of good and evil. I worried about their devotion to Julie, a product of both, but, I feared, more a Compton than a MacDonald.

That combination of Caesar and Pope, old man Compton.

His evil genius, his need to control. There, that was the problem. At the end of his life, he wouldn't let go and there was no order of succession. I remembered Suzanne's look of triumph when the old man tapped her to work with me. Her triumph and Eddie's look of chagrin.

Out of control? A bloody interregnum—a fight for succession even though the old man was not yet gone.

Interregnum might explain Arjuna's murder. Whichever of the clan remained alive at the end to take over Jacob Compton's empire would be the heir and the guilty party. But what about old Mrs. MacDonald? How could she have stood in anyone's way? What on earth did she have to do with the Compton family fortunes? It just didn't wash.

I stirred myself. Heidi was looking at me thoughtfully, an envelope in her hand. "Your money," she said laying the envelope on the table between us.

The joss stick had burned out. The candle flame rose like an elongated kernel of corn. It was getting late.

"I've got to go."

"You figured it out," Heidi said, embarrassing me again.

"You're crazy," I snorted and stood.

"No. You're crazy. Trust it." Heidi and the dragon embraced me.

At the door, Heidi took hold of my sleeve. "Watch out for that Suzanne woman," she said. "And when you go back to Nova Scotia, take someone with you. Take Sister Pat."

Chapter 17

I dithered at the corner of Broadway and a hundred and seventh. It was too late to fly back to Maine. The wad of bills Heidi had given me made a comforting bulge at my groin, but I didn't want to blow it on a hotel.

I was afraid of Suzanne. Not slit-my-throat afraid, but what Heidi might call lack-of-self-esteem afraid. If I were to see Suzanne right then, before long I would begin to babble about what I suspected. Heidi might like my crazy, but it wouldn't rate high on a Compton scale of preferences.

A taxi slid to the curb in front of me. "Know what you're doin', lady?" the cabby called out the passenger window.

"Yeah," I said. I gave him the address in Harlem of the Emmaus Hotel. Surprisingly, he didn't try to argue me out of it.

I spent the night in the women's dorm. Didn't get much sleep, the Avenue comes to life at night and, warm as it was, they left all the windows open. But I was out of there by four, and a little after seven my 'Business Connection', a toy-like plane seating ten, landed at Bangor International. I called Pat. She said she'd pick me up as soon as Barney got back with the truck.

"When'll that be?"

"You know Barney," she said.

"Not really. Where is she?"

"Monte Cassino."

"With Clara?"

No response. Translation: Barney was with the magnetic Santa Clara and might not get home for hours.

"Come with me to Nova Scotia," I invited. "Pack. I'll pick you up in forty-five minutes."

"I thought you needed a lift from the airport."

"I'll come in a pumpkin, be ready." I hung up before she could protest.

Budget Rental had a Shadow they were willing to let me have on the strength of a credit card. Half an hour later I bumped into the Cloister dooryard.

Who will milk Rosie? feed the chickens? shingle the shed? All her questions I answered with "Barney will." Then I urged, "Hurry! We need to get to Halifax before five, and they're an hour ahead of us."

While Pat got her toothbrush and comb together, I called information and then the Nova Scotia Department of Vital Statistics. I explained what I wanted and asked whether I could stop by later in the day to pick up the information. Cordial as a jeweler at Tiffany's, the clerk said I surely could, and that they closed at five.

We hit the Angus MacDonald Bridge at 4:15 p.m., Atlantic time. The nice toll-taker told us how to get on Gottingen Street and where to turn off. The information the clerk at Vital Statistics had for me confirmed my suspicions.

"You just made it," he observed. And then he apologized. "I'm afraid I couldn't find anything for you."

I smiled and replied, "I didn't expect you would."

What the clerk hadn't been able to find was a date for the demise of Jacob Compton's wife, Anna Maria Zuccollo. If she was dead, she hadn't died in Nova Scotia. I asked the clerk where the Halifax psychiatric hospital was located.

"In Dartmouth," he said. "Across the river." He supplied directions and added, ominously, "You can't miss it."

Pat, dressed in her traveling costume, a short-skirted habit, crisply black and white, asked, when we hit the pavement outside, "What was that all about?"

On the long drive up, I had explained as much as I could to

her, starting with why I was no longer with Suzanne. It took until Moncton to settle her mind on this point, in part because I first had to explain about Heidi. Pat and I had never discussed my past, which I think of as speckled—drab with spots of color, mostly purple, in it. I hadn't thought she would be amused, and she had never pried.

After I explained that Heidi's parting words to me had been, "Stay away from that Suzanne, and don't go to Nova Scotia alone. Take Pat," Pat said thoughtfully, "I would like to meet Heidi sometime."

"Yeah," I said. "Next time we're in New York."

"I'd rather," said Pat, "she come to visit us in Maine."

Us? As in Pat and me? I didn't dare to ask.

All I had told Pat about the reason for our trip to Vital Statistics was that I wanted to find out whether Eddie MacDonald's birth certificate listed a father—it didn't—and when Mrs. Compton had died. She hadn't.

"What's with the psychiatric hospital?" asked Pat.

I explained, haltingly, as we worked our way through the rush hour traffic to Dartmouth, my thoughts on the Compton Interregnum.

"What I couldn't understand is why this illegitimate child, Eddie MacDonald, who the old man disposed of in the St. Therese orphanage, and then shipped his mother off to India— why Eddie later was taken into the heart of the Compton family. Both his mother and him. Eddie was taken in to the extent that when his liaison with Denise was discovered, old Jacob Compton forced him to marry her. And then, when the marriage hit the rocks, the old man, according to Heidi, made Eddie bring the baby back with him to Canada."

This long speech almost cost us our lives. I got so excited I didn't notice a twenty-wheeler intent on beating me to the toll booth.

"Wait till we're out of the traffic," Pat pleaded, handing me a dollar bill to pay the toll.

"Don't you have any Canadian money?"

"Where would I get Canadian money?"

"That will do," the young woman in the booth intervened.

I thanked her. The change was Canadian. Pat put it in the ashtray for next time.

In the hospital parking lot, I continued my speculations.

"It seemed like old Jacob Compton wasn't happy with the succession, that is with his oldest son, David. There's something feudal about him and the way he treats his off-spring. He intended for his first-born to continue to make money. That's David, the man you knew as Arjuna. I guess from what you told me, David/Arjuna did make money with his Buddhism, and intended to make a lot more from real estate development around his temple complexes. There's another of those going up in Nova Scotia, by the way. But Arjuna was a rascal.

"The second son was to be a great intellectual. He publishes slim volumes of poetry. They're well reviewed. But it's the Compton background. The poems aren't really very good, and he's more like someone acting the part than the genuine article."

Pat nodded. "Long hair?" she asked.

"Good God, no. Bohemianism isn't on in that family. No, Paul wears three piece suits and his hair is nicely gray at the ears. Walter Pidgeon."

"So, who takes over? Pearl?"

"That's the question. They seem to be deciding the succession the way the Borgias did. A little kidnaping, a little knifing. Let's not eat our soup until the dog has had a taste."

"Get outta here!"

"Suit yourself," I laughed.

"It doesn't make sense, though," Pat said thoughtfully. She seemed reluctant to leave the warm coziness of the car. The hospital, like loony bins everywhere, was bleak and forbidding. "Is Arthur/Jesus crazy enough to think he could take over? I mean, even if he killed everyone else? And, anyway, isn't he too crazy to want to? If he thinks he's Jesus."

"It's not Arthur I'm worried about," I said.

"Suzanne?" said Pat, hopefully, I think.

"You know," I said, "I don't believe Arjuna and Julie were lovers."

"No," said Pat. "I never thought so."

She looked embarrassed. I helped her out: "You thought he was making it with Arthur/Jesus." Pat squirmed. "Which would be worse in the Compton roster of mortal sins?" I said. "Heterosexual incest with your niece or homosexual incest with your nephew?"

I started to open the door. "Actually, I suspect he was innocent of either involvement. For all his shenanigans, I suspect Arjuna was rather conventional. He had an instinct for money-making. His Buddhism was always connected to real estate speculation. Like the old man's charity, which, I imagine includes tax exempt slums, and...." I stopped, afraid to wound Pat's religious sensibilities.

"Oh say it," she snapped. "I wasn't born yesterday, Brigid. I do read the newspapers. Vatican gold and limousines aren't bought with money from the Sunday collection."

I had been going to say "brothels," but I let it ride.

We were silent approaching the looming mass of the Nova Scotia Hospital. Arjuna's shenanigans and Julie's were what had prompted me to pursue inquiries concerning the absent Compton matriarch. That there were no memorials to her, just the conventional story that she had died in childbirth, puzzled me. I would expect at the least a small altar, perhaps a perpetual flame. But there was nothing, not even a portrait.

Then there was the odd circumstance that after Julie's birth, Eddie MacDonald had been called back to the bosom of the Compton family. And Pearl, too, had been elevated to a position of leadership within the Compton charitable—read tax exempt, and not much scrutinized—conglomerate.

Heidi had been certain that when she wrote to Jacob Compton about Eddie, she had been writing to Eddie's father. That suggested a line of thought to me. By the time his legitimate sons, David and Paul, were thirty, it must have become apparent to the Old Man that the one wasn't able and the other was unstable. At this juncture, Heidi's letter arrived with the news that Jacob's other son, the child of his liaison with the servant girl, Pearl MacDonald, was alive and doing well in New York City, and was about to become a father.

What would someone as powerful and controlling as old Jacob Compton do, I mused, under these circumstances? Bring Eddie back home, obviously. Eddie and another possible heir, the new baby, Julie. Too bad that both children from that generation were girls. Back then there were some things that just couldn't be controlled, not even by the Vatican.

Girls, and one at least, a little crazy. Suzanne seemed to be a little crazy about me, which was crazy. Julie was crazy period.

"A bloody interregnum," I muttered.

"Interregnum?" said Pat. We were approaching the reception desk. A burly nurse made to bar our way.

"Old man Compton hasn't picked a successor," I said. "And he plays with them. It's dangerous."

I said to the burly nurse that we were there to visit Anna Maria Zuccollo Compton. He seemed glad. On the way to her room he confided that no one but her cousin had ever been to visit her before.

"Her cousin?" I asked.

"Yes," he said. "He must be nearly a hundred now. Comes with an attendant, in a wheel chair. Very faithful he is. Every Saturday afternoon. Does you good to see it."

At 85, Anna Maria Zuccollo Compton was still a great beauty. Her hair, thin now and silver, was curly, like Suzanne's, her sloe eyes tilted and dark like Arjuna's, her mouth, no longer full and ripe, had retained the sensuous modeling of Suzanne's mouth, the same Botticelli curves I first had seen in Julia's lips. These were features I had seen, too, in Old Man Compton. The children and grandchildren of this couple bore such a strong family resemblance because they were working from a limited gene pool. Anna Maria was the old man's cousin, as well as his wife.

She smiled vacantly at us. She sat in a rocker by the open window, an afghan over her knees. Except for being beautiful she might have been Whistler's mother. Except for her beauty and the great emptiness in her eyes.

Empty, but not hostile. Anna Maria Zuccollo Compton was like a bell jar, her composure as serene and transparent as glass.

One sensed in her an inner presence so fragile it would shatter in an everyday environment. Returning our greeting with a smile and a nod, she turned again to her window. The smile was small and shy, like a young girl's smile for company. Her head began to nod as if she heard a melody, a serenade. A lover in the twilight wooing.

That smile and nod were the only acknowledgment of our presence that Anna Maria Zuccollo Compton ever made. After a half hour we rose, Pat and I, like Bedouins, and slipped away.

Charles, old Mr. Compton's doppelgänger, met us on the steps going out.

"Mr. Compton would be greatly flattered," he said, "if you," his nod took in both Pat and me, "would be his guests this evening. He suggested that if you haven't eaten, he would have a high tea prepared." He gestured toward the car. "I'll telephone your preferences."

Head cocked, hands clasped at his chest, he looked like a head waiter trying to conciliate some very special VIPs. The only way he could conciliate me was by booking it out of there. "Not tonight, Charles," I said.

He took my arm and in an undertone he said, "Please don't make trouble, Mrs. Donovan."

My eyes followed the direction of his nod, discreet as a Sotheby auctioneer's. Two attendants lounged in the doorway of the hospital. Each held a garment, a jacket, white and with extremely long sleeves. I had seen jackets like that before. When they carted Alicia off to St. Elizabeth's. Alicia, the woman Heidi thinks I left her for. The attendants in their white tunics had wrapped Alicia in just such a jacket. The only way to keep her from shredding her skin. DTs. She thought bugs were crawling on her. The arms are long so they can be tied around you. After they put the jacket on, they lock you in a padded cell. Pat and I might not be crazy when they locked us up, but after a couple shots of Thorazine in our arms or butt, we'd look certifiable. We'd feel it too.

I turned to Pat. "High tea? I'm hungry, aren't you?"

She looked mulish. Discreet as a kid on a Bronx street corner,

I hooked my thumb at the two attendants. Pat's look changed from anger to alarm. Before it could swing back to anger I said, "Pat, let me introduce you to Charles, Mr. Compton's assistant."

Looking up at Charles, who still held my arm, I said, "Charles, I'm sorry I didn't get your last name. I would like you to meet my friend, Sister Pat."

My cotillion teacher in Panama would have been proud of me.

Chapter 18

On the way to the Compton mansion, I drew a genealogy of the family trees. As much for my benefit as for Pat's. And as much to keep us cool as anything. I used Heidi's nomenclature.

Heavenly City (MacDonald)
Angus-Pearl
Faith   Hope   Charity (Pearl)
Eddie-Denise
Julie, Arthur

Earthly City (Compton)
Jacob-Anna Maria Zuccollo
Paul—(m. Lucy)   David (Arjuna)
Suzanne

I made two notations under these:
Jacob Compton—Pearl MacDonald
Eddie MacDonald
And
David/Arjuna—Eddie MacDonald
Compton Brother's, Ltd.

Jacob Compton's mouth. I hadn't noticed before. Lorenzo de Medici—that bust of him in the National Gallery—he has a mouth like old man Compton's. Fuller, because Lorenzo was younger when the likeness was made. Crueler, maybe because he was a Medici. But old man Compton, like his wife, Anna Maria, like Suzanne and like Julia, had lips that were full and sensuous.

"You really are her cousin," I said to him. He nodded.

Charles had brought us up the sweeping curve of the marble staircase to the comforts of the second floor. Our repast was served in the intimacy of what must have been Jacob Compton's bedroom. Like Suzanne's, his was large enough to accommodate several groupings of arm chairs and lounges. Charles served tea on a balcony overlooking the topiary zoo. It would be dark soon and the large greenery animals, the elephant and the giraffe, threw long shadows. While we ate our way through the salads and cheeses, the patés and little sausages, Jacob Compton lavished on Pat the charm that he recently had bestowed on me. Like me, she responded. It was over coffee afterwards that I threw in my remark about his blood relationship to his wife, Anna Maria Zuccollo.

"That's not material," he said. His beautiful lips smiled, but not his eyes.

"Murder is material," I replied testily.

"Tsk, tsk" said he.

"Why did you have us brought here?" asked Pat suddenly, as if she just then recalled that we hadn't come to tea of our own free will exactly.

The old man nodded, almost imperceptibly, to Charles who began to clear away the dishes.

"Will you join me," he said to Pat, "in a brandy? It is very choice. For you, Brigid," he turned to me and his smile glowed briefly like a benediction, "I have a special treat."

They each had a delicate thimble of Courvoisier. Mine was a Kahlua, rich, satisfying, and he assured me, "You could never regret it."

"About why you brought us here," Pat said again. The shadows of the beasts outdoors had dissolved in the approaching night.

"I thought," the old man said, "you might have some questions you would like to ask me."

"Just like that?" I asked, surprised.

"Why not, Brigid? We're friends," he said and smiled his blessing on me.

"Do I get three?"

"You get as many as you like," he replied serenely.

My first question was to ask why he was willing to answer my questions. He was doing it, he said, because it was the right thing to do. Prodded, he continued to explain that he had hired me, through Pearl, to find Julia and Arthur, and then, unforgivably, had put roadblocks in my way.

"Worse than unforgivable." He chuckled. "Stupid."

He looked like a gnome, slight and mischievous, and, for all his littleness, quite powerful enough to guard his hoarded treasure.

"Stupid?" I challenged.

He reached across the newly cleared table to squeeze my hand. "Well, I expected you would be detained in New York until Charles managed to straighten things out up here. But then the phone call from the hospital this evening that Anna Maria had visitors. You are a woman of great resourcefulness, Brigid."

He continued to hold my hand in his. It felt good—dry and warm, spare and capable.

"How did you shake Suzanne?" he asked.

"Is this your question or mine?" I replied.

"I'm sorry."

"No. I think you know the answer. Count it as my second question."

"You may ask as many questions as you want."

"So you keep saying. But you seem to be dodging this one. How was it Suzanne didn't keep a better eye on me?"

With my hand still in his, he turned to Pat and said, "This one is something, isn't she." To me he said, "I am not playing games with you, Brigid Donovan. I don't know. My instructions to Suzanne were very simple, to stay with you until things here were settled. I was surprised to hear that you were at Nova Scotia Hospital. Wasn't I, Charles?"

Charles dutifully nodded. The old man looked at me enquiringly.

"Suzanne and I parted when I went to St. Elizabeth's, where Denise, your daughter-in-law, died."

He didn't blink at the daughter-in-law. I went on. "She said she was going to an address on Central Park West. Three hundred. You have a pied-a-terre there she said. She probably didn't expect me to find out much, but the address they gave me at St. Elizabeth's—of the person to notify—turned out to be an old friend. I went there and from her place I flew directly back to Maine."

Looking back, I think the old man threw me a life line then, gave me a sporting chance in the game. At the time I barely took notice. He murmured absently, "Heidi McCarren."

"Yes," I confirmed.

"Even if you're counting," he smiled, "you have another question. Maybe two. I don't know why Suzanne didn't keep better track of you. Maybe, as you say, she simply miscalculated."

I asked the big one. "Where are Julia and Arthur?"

"Charles," the old man said, and nodded, barely.

Charles, his voice dropping Zeus-like from above, said, "I believe, sir, they have been located in Montreal. Our operatives traced their vehicle there. They seem to be registered in the Motel Quebec."

"Believe? Seem?" said the old man.

"It isn't confirmed, sir."

Jacob Compton shrugged at me. "Tomorrow we shall know more. The rascals will be apprehended. Before the police find them, I hope." He tsked a couple of times.

"Rascals?" said Pat incredulously.

"They have been very naughty," the old man said.

"You don't think Arthur is responsible for either murder? Your son David's or Mrs. MacDonald's?" I asked. "That's what Pearl thinks" I added. "And Suzanne."

He shook his head sadly. "Arthur—and Julia!—are guilty of having come under the influence of a very charming but unscrupulous man. My son David, Brigid, whom you never met. Did you know him, Sister? No. By reputation, perhaps. Yes."

Jacob Compton then ruefully explained that Pearl had, that

morning, discovered in Arjuna's handwriting, a set of ransom notes like those delivered by Arthur, aka Jesus.

"We believe," he explained, "that Arjuna decided to stage this kidnapping of young Julia so that she could collect her own ransom. Pearl said that Julia was becoming restive there in—is it Surry?—Maine. And, except for her so-called stigmata, she really had no means to achieve financial independence."

Her situation depended on the Old Man's good will. Not a happy situation for a budding sociopath. Julie was stuck and it made her unhappy. It would make anyone unhappy.

"It's something my son...." Here the old man paused and shook his head sadly. "That *I* should have a son who became a Buddhist! Arjuna!" He spat out the word as though it were tangible and bitter. "It's something he would have found amusing to do—stage a kidnapping, then deliver the ransom money to the putative victim who could then disappear with it."

He shook his head in disapproval, but a glint in those gnomish eyes suggested he didn't think the scheme was without a redeeming feature, sauce probably. Old Man Compton, I had already noticed, preferred his saucier offspring. I imagined beneath his disapproval, he adored Julia. Arjuna, though, must have gone too far. Where Arjuna was concerned, the old man did not seem to be a grieving father. I wondered briefly if he could have been jealous. There was no doubting Pearl's fondness for Arjuna. Perhaps, in the old man's eyes, she had been too fond?

"That explains the so-called kidnapping," I said. "But what about the murders?"

"Brigid, my dear, about them I don't even care to speculate. It is best to let the police in Surry—here the RCMPs—let them handle the murders. They're trained. For us, we can look into the peccadilloes of our own family. But not murder." He squeezed my hand. His brow wrinkled with regret. "That, dear Brigid, is for trained investigators. Don't be offended."

I brushed offense away like flies on a summer day. "Of course not," I said.

Pat said, "I think we should be going." She looked at her watch.

"Oh," said the old man, "I won't hear of your going. You must stay. Charles will show you to your room. Because, Brigid," his bright eyes bore earnestly into my own, "it is familiar, I had them prepare Suzanne's room for you." He said to Pat "We put in a bed for you, Sister. I'm sure you will find it comfortable."

He lifted his head slightly and said, "Charles, will you show these two young women to their room."

As we followed dutifully behind Charles, I reflected that however conventionally polite the phrases were, when old Jacob Compton said he wouldn't hear of our going and that we must stay, that is exactly what he meant. At the door of Suzanne's apartment, Charles wished us a pleasant night and then he said, "I believe you will not want anything. But if you should, please ring the bell-pull by the door. A woman will come immediately to help you. Her name is Belle. She is my wife."

When he closed the door, I heard a key turn in the lock. Pat heard it, too. She tried the door. It wouldn't open. We were locked in for the night, so it seemed. Pat reached for the bell-pull.

"What are you doing?"

"Getting out of here!"

"Hold on," I said. "There may be a better way."

The back way Suzanne and I had used to escape on the night of the dinner party began in the dressing room. "Come with me," I whispered to Pat, drawing her along behind me.

The small chamber held a vanity and a lounge. Across the back stood a paneled cedar screen, each panel ornately carved with elephants, tigers and other exotic animals. The screen masked an unused servants' door leading to the kitchen, and to freedom. I pulled Pat behind the screen to show her.

"You think that's unlocked?" she asked skeptically.

"It was two days ago," I replied.

"Well, let's go then," she said, too preoccupied with escaping to inquire how I knew.

"No, let's wait a while. Till everyone's in bed."

"At least see if it's unlocked."

I held my breath as I tried. The door opened easily and noiselessly. It was dark on the landing. "Got a flashlight?" I whispered.

"As a matter of fact," said Pat. "Nuns and Boy Scouts, we're both prepared."

Her flashlight was only a two-inch long one on her key chain, but it was enough to get us out of the house without falling or bumping into anything. We waited in the dark until after midnight to leave.

Barring child birth, that wait was the longest two hours of my life. I was too tired to sleep, though Pat dozed off. I spent the time worrying. For all his apparent frankness, I trusted nothing the old man had told me. If Charles said that Arthur and Julie had been traced to Montreal, I took it as given they were not even in Quebec Province. But my distrust was deeper and broader than that, it was global. Sitting at the window, staring out at the rosy glow of the night sky, I tried to recall every statement the old man had made, so that I could examine it systematically for the lie.

He had told Suzanne, he said, to stick with me.

He was surprised to hear we were at the Nova Scotia Hospital visiting his wife.

The kidnapping had nothing to do with the murders.

The kidnapping was a family peccadillo.

I remembered then that he had murmured Heidi's name. All I had said was that the name I got at St. Elizabeth's was an old friend of mine and that I had gone to her. Old Jacob Compton interjected her name, Heidi McCarren. How had he known it was Heidi's name Denise had listed as the person to notify? For how long had he known it? She had written him only twice.

Perhaps it was only conjecture on his part. Heidi, after all, had written two portentous letters to him regarding Denise and about Arthur. Had he thrown in Heidi's name only to confirm it?

I tried to recall the moment exactly. At the time, it had seemed a subtle warning. But I no longer trusted my impressions where Jacob Compton was concerned, for I had come to realize, with chagrin, that I wanted to believe he liked me.

But say it was a warning: what had he been warning me of? Had it been his way to let me know that the trip to New York and my flight back to Maine was all a set-up? That Suzanne had accompanied me in order, like a sheep-dog, to herd me?

If all that were so, what was I to make of the escape hatch nicely left open for Pat and me? Suzanne told me that the door had not been used for years except for the use she made of it to get out of the house undetected. She said no one even remembered that it was there. But I doubted Jacob Compton was unaware of anything in his domain.

Not that my paranoid fears mattered. Pat and I did not intend to spend the night in the Compton mansion. Besides, I was sure I knew where Arthur/Jesus and Julie were, had been ever since Mrs. MacDonald's murder five days before. Five days. A long time for a desperate person, who has already killed twice, to refrain from killing again.

At one, I woke Pat. "How could you sleep?" I asked. She mumbled something about a pure heart and needing to brush her teeth.

We made it downstairs and out the back without any trouble. No different from when Suzanne and I had done the same just three nights before. Still, I felt uneasy.

Between rows of savage beasts—lion, gorilla, elephant—stirring restlessly and growling in the cold night wind, Pat and I, hand-in-hand, made our way through the grounds to the alley.

"Do you know where we are?" asked Pat.

I didn't, but I knew better than to let on. There was a tremor in Pat's voice that spoke of fear.

"Left," I said firmly. And left we went.

The alley debauched on a tree-lined boulevard, well-lit but empty except for a van parked on the far side. The van looked familiar. But, unexpected and unexplainable, I dismissed the familiarity.

"Now what?" said Pat. The fear was gone, the fear of being caught before we made our get-away, but her voice sounded brittle still, and through the touch of her hand I could feel how rigid her body was, bracing itself against unknown dangers.

"This way," I said with factitious confidence, steering her toward the right and, with luck, the campus of Dalhousie University.

We hadn't gone more than a dozen paces when the stutter of

an engine starting broke the stillness of the night. Pat stiffened and squeezed against me. I pulled her close, my arm around her waist.

"Keep walking," I said. We did, but haltingly like two blind people without canes.

As we moved on, the van shifted into gear. Tires squealed in a racing start. Maybe a couple of kids necking, I thought, and the thought made me aware of Pat's closeness. She smelled of lavender, like Suzanne. Suzanne's lavender, I realized.

"You smell good," I whispered in her ear.

She pulled away from me. Tartly she said, "I thought you might like it."

Was that a come-on, or a put-down? I was trying to relocate her hand in the folds of her habit when we heard a car approach from behind. We looked back together. It was the van again. Mesmerized we stood and watched it slow and stop beside us. Suzanne leaned across, and through the open window invited, "Hop in, you two. You look frozen."

Chapter 19

I guess I could have said no thanks, we're enjoying our walk. But somehow I didn't think it mattered much whether we joined Suzanne in the van or not. Ever since our encounter with Charles the evening before, we had not been free agents. I couldn't imagine Suzanne threatening us as Charles had. There were no guys with straight jackets in the back of her van. But I could imagine all kinds of back-up if we turned down Suzanne's invitation. Hopping in as she suggested seemed the sensible thing to do. Not that I trusted her. I knew whatever fondness she had for me would not count for much against the Compton fortune and the old man's wishes. Still. Better than Charles, better than life in a loony bin.

So I said—all smiles and good cheer—"Hey! What brings you here?" And to Pat I said, "What do you know! It's Suzanne." Suzanne, whose lavender water you're wearing. Pulling Pat to me, I whispered, "I think we better go along with this."

"Brigid!" she hissed. "The things I let you get me into!"

I pushed Pat into the van ahead of me, afraid she'd take off if I weren't careful. "Suzanne, Pat," I said by way of introductions.

Suzanne offered her hand, but Pat suddenly became busy straightening her coif. Pat said, "I believe we spoke on the phone."

"Oh, right!" said Suzanne laughing, both hands again on the wheel. "Where to?" she said.

"I believe," said Pat, "it is called the Nova Scotia Hospital. It's

142

across the river. If you can get me to the bridge, I can direct you from there."

"Um, Pat," I said, "Suzanne is from Halifax."

"I see. Then she doesn't need my help."

Yeah.

On our way Suzanne asked why the hospital. I explained about the car. I explained about Charles and our invitation to tea. "We could hardly say no," Pat interjected, leaving me to tell the rest.

"Well," said Suzanne, after I had described the two men on the hospital stairs, long-sleeved white jackets dangling in their hands, "I doubt that your car will be there. It's probably back home in the garage." But she agreed to check it out.

She was right. The little blue Shadow was gone. "Where to next, boss?" she asked. She and Pat both turned and looked at me expectantly.

The street in front of the hospital was deserted. The yellow glow of street lights cast a jaundiced pall on the sky. The window where Anna Maria Zuccollo Compton had spent a lifetime silently staring was blind. I felt a chill of despair. "Scotsburn," I said. "And I think we should hurry."

The moon, when we pulled into the farm yard, was almost as bright and as full as five nights before, and in about the same position. Longing to be wrong in my fears, I looked up under the eaves of the barn, hoping against hope to see moonlight reflected in a window pane there. But no such luck. The looming hulk of the barn was dark. Dark just like the huddled berm house. Dark as a grave.

Dark, but not silent. The goats in the barn bleated a symphony of discontent, and, as we drew close on foot, we could hear the syncopated mutter of unhappy chickens. Enough moonlight filtered through the windows so we could see that the goats' mangers were empty and their udders full.

"Where's the light," Pat exclaimed. "These poor things have to be milked. Now!"

I put a restraining hand on her shoulder. "Shh!" I said. "Wait

143

a minute. How long do you think it's been since they were milked last?"

"What difference does that make?" she said curtly. "They're suffering." She shook herself loose from my grip and started toward the light switch mounted on the beam that framed the doorway.

"Wait!" I said. "Don't turn on that light!"

Pat ignored me. But Suzanne suddenly came to life. She threw herself between Pat and the door. For a moment it looked like the first casualties would be on our side. From friendly fire, if you could call Pat and Suzanne friendly. Maybe they weren't even on the same side.

"Didn't you hear Brigid?" Suzanne hissed. She held both Pat's wrists.

It was touch and go whether the two of them would land on the floor in a no-holds-barred wrestling match. But Pat restrained herself. Over her shoulder she asked, her arms rigid in Suzanne's tight grasp, "Brigid, they need to be milked, why not turn on the light?"

"Let her go," I said to Suzanne. "I'm afraid, Pat, we may have a problem here. Like Arthur and Julie."

For a moment we were silent, the only sound in the barn the unhappy bleating of the goats, which had become more urgent with our coming.

Pat's sigh re-animated our tableau. She said, "Well, you two do what you need to do. I have to milk these poor creatures. I can do it in the dark."

She turned away. I sensed in her turning a withdrawal. A withdrawal not just from whatever terrible prospect awaited Suzanne and me in the berm house, but a withdrawal from me, from that fragile bond the two of us had spun over the years.

"Pat!" I whispered. "Wait!" But the black of her habit had dissolved in the gloom.

Suzanne grabbed my hand. "Let her go," she said.

The weather had turned colder. A blustery wind, smelling of rain, wailed intermittently. It looked, in the moonlight, to be a ghost fluttering at the door of the farmhouse, but it was only one of Julie's veils caught on a splinter of wood.

Suzanne and I hesitated on the threshold. The only sound we could hear was the wind. "Hello!" Suzanne cried into the dark. But nothing stirred. Nothing except Julie's futile finery.

"They're gone," she said.

"Maybe. Turn on the light."

The room seemed to spring at us: the shining steel equipment hooked neatly to the beam, the drying herbs, the silent spinning wheel and loom. I didn't see them at first. The television, its sightless eye, quivering and gray like a cataract, drew my attention to the corner where Hope had been busy working when I first visited. Both sisters were there, on the floor, in each other's arms. Hope seemed to be comforting Faith as if in the end it was the stronger sister who had given way to despair.

"Oh, dear God!" Suzanne beside me breathed. "Poor Julie."

They hadn't been dead long. Not like their mother when I discovered her. Except for the blood, they might have been sleeping. I sank to the stool where Hope had sat when she would spin.

"He's crazy!" said Suzanne. She seemed to be milking her hands. "We knew he was crazy. But Granddad said he was harmless. He said the kidnapping was only a joke. He said—"

"Shut up," I said.

Suzanne began to cry.

I went to the window and looked out across the moon-bleached landscape toward the barn. There, high up in the eaves where I had noticed it before, a light wavered, but it wasn't the moon.

I knew with a wrenching certainty that Pat was up there. What I didn't know was whether she was still alive. I turned to leave.

"Where're you going?" Suzanne cried.

"To the barn," I said.

"Don't go. They'll kill you."

There was something other than fear, something more than mere reaction in her voice.

"They?" I said. "They'll kill me? Not Arthur? Who's 'they,' Suzanne?"

She didn't answer. I took a step in her direction. On the table lay a knife. I picked it up and moved in on her.

"You better start telling me the truth," I said. "Who's this 'they' you're afraid of?"

Tears had left a forlorn trail down her cheeks. She grimaced, meaning it for a smile. "Put down the knife, Brigid," she said. "'It's...it's ugly."

She was right, it was. A butcher knife, long and sharp and bloody. I let it go. I saw there was blood on my hand and tried to rub it off. But like Lady Macbeth's, my hands would not come clean.

"Now look what you've done," said Suzanne, crying and laughing and pointing her finger at my bloody trousers. "Just look at you."

"Who's going to kill me," I said again. " Tell me, damn you."

"Arthur," she said. "Arthur, of course. Who else?"

But I knew she was lying. I turned again toward the door.

"You can forget about your precious nun," she flung at me.

My hands were on her neck and I didn't remember turning, couldn't remember covering the space between us. The hard pressure of my thumbs on the bones of her jaw woke me. "You're choking me," she gibbered.

"I will if you don't tell me what you know," I said; and, for a moment, I think I meant it. So did she.

She wrenched my hands away—I didn't resist—and moved past me toward the table. She sank onto a chair, wilted, her head buried in her hands. Only her hair, black and glinting with fine silver wires, was unsubdued. I joined her, roughly pulling a chair up beside her.

"I'm going to count to three," I said. "If you haven't told me what you know, we're going together to the barn." On the table, under her eyes, I thrust the bloody blade of the butcher knife.

"One."

"Oh, Brigid," she sighed. "Put the knife away. It's too bad about Pat. I really am sorry."

"What's too bad? God damn it talk to me."

Only the finest thread of common sense held me in the berm

house, and it was fraying rapidly.

Suzanne raised her head, her eyes seeking mine, seeking to hold them in hers, a smile wavering on those sensuous lips. She looked stricken and old, alluring—with her writhing curls—as Medusa.

"Grandfather didn't expect you to come with anyone." She said it apologetically. Like, 'Sorry we didn't set a place at the table.'

"I brought the ransom money. It's in the van," she said. "I'll show you. Maybe if you left now...." Her voice trailed off.

"Suzanne," I said savagely, "tell me now what your grandfather told you to do."

"Just stick with you. That's all."

"In New York."

"In New York.... In New York he said to let you go alone to St. Elizabeth's."

I knew there was more. "What's happened to Pat?"

"Arthur." The syllables swelled into a wail.

"Did you know Arthur would be here?"

She shook her head. The misery in those oriental eyes looked real, the misery and the fear. "I think we should take the ransom money and go now," she said.

"When your grandfather sent you here," I said, certain that Suzanne had been told to intercept Pat and me when we escaped from the mansion, "did he know Arthur would be here? Did he know about this?" I gestured toward the huddled bodies on the floor.

The fear in Suzanne's eyes deepened. "Oh no," she said. But her despair gave the lie away. Suzanne realized that whatever Granddad had said, he knew the trap he had ordered Suzanne to walk into with Brigid Donovan, ace detective, in tow.

"Brigid, Arthur's crazy. He's killed four people." Her voice wavered. "That we know of."

"You don't want to help your cousin, Julie?"

I couldn't keep the sarcasm from my voice. It stung a quick retort from Suzanne. "Be my guest, Wonder Woman."

"No, you be mine." I pulled her roughly to her feet. "You're coming with me."

She tried to pull away. "Why?" she cried. "It's too late. You know it's too late. Brigid, take the ransom money and go. We'll go together."

The ransom money. She kept harping on it. Why?

"That's Granddad speaking, isn't it?" For I suddenly knew—with a clarity beyond reason—that Suzanne had been instructed to link the ransom money to me. I couldn't imagine why, and right then I didn't care.

"Okay," I said. "Lets take a look at the money."

Suzanne's relief burst upon her face like the sun breaking through. "Good!" she cried, "Let's get out of here!"

Outside, clouds obscured the moon, which had slipped quite low in the sky, but light from milky clouds and stars overhead made it easy to see. The window in the eaves was lighted still. Inside the barn a small star seemed to twinkle in the straw. I caught Suzanne's arm and pulled her with me toward the barn door.

"Where're you going?"she said.

"Before we go, I have to find Pat."

"It's too late," she pleaded.

The star was Pat's key-chain flashlight. I used it to look around. The goats seemed content enough, busy at their mangers eating, their bags no longer swollen. A bucket of milk stood nearly full on a shelf by the door. Whatever had happened to Pat happened after she had cared for the creatures.

The only sounds were night sounds, barn sounds, the sound of the wind and of Suzanne snuffling. Then faintly, ever so faintly, I heard the sound of straw stirring as someone came slowly toward us. I doused the light.

Chapter 20

"It's you," Pat breathed.

"Oh Jesus!" Suzanne beside me moaned.

"No, he's upstairs," said Pat wryly, resurrecting me. Her voice, her humor.

"Hi," I said.

"You're all blood," she whispered.

"Yeah. I know." Hurriedly I explained the shambles in the berm house.

"They're upstairs," said Pat. "I was going up to investigate when I heard you outside. I dropped my flashlight."

Suzanne said, "Let's get out of here."

"What about Julie?" I asked.

Suzanne had grabbed my right arm and was headed out the door. Pat, my left bicep held securely, moved back toward the ladder leading up into the eaves. "Hold on!" I whispered. Together, neither turning, they said, "Come on, Brigid!"

"Wait! I have a plan," I pleaded.

Because Pat slackened her hold momentarily, our little group floundered out into the moonlit barnyard. Above us the light in the window went out. We were clearly visible to whoever up there was looking down.

"Quick! Pat, don't argue, to the van," I urged. The Old Man's silent attendant, his doppelgänger, Charles, stepped out of the shadows. The gun he held was big and black.

"Charles! thank God, you're here!" Suzanne cried, running toward him.

Precise as a pendulum, Charles' gun hand swung down and up. The gun caught Suzanne's jaw. She dropped and didn't move. Charles stood back from the door. With a short, butler bow he motioned us to get in. "Miss Donovan, I must ask you to drive," he said. "Sister, if you would let her get in first." He made a fussy face and said, "There has been so much violence, Mr. Compton hopes that more will not be necessary." He lowered his eyes modestly toward the gun in his hand.

"You don't want to use that," I said. "The weapon you want is in the house."

"Tsk tsk," said Charles, the dog resembling its master. "I trust I won't need any weapon at all."

"What about her?" I gestured toward Suzanne. "It's cold, it might rain. You can't leave her lying there like that."

"The sooner we go, the sooner help can be sent for her."

I climbed in. Pat started to follow. I heard her breath escape like air from a punctured tire. I looked back. The eye of the gun met mine not six inches away. "Get in," said Charles.

"I'll direct you," he said, settling himself in the corner, the gun held steadily pointed at me. As I let out the clutch, he turned and fired two shots at the ground where the bodies of Pat and Suzanne lay.

"Steady there," he said calmly as I hit the brakes and the van swerved off the track. I felt the hard barrel of the gun press against my ribs. "Steady there, Miss Donovan. Getting the two of us killed won't bring back your friends. You drive steady now." And somehow I managed to.

Somewhere recently I had read that survival is a state of mind. My state of my mind that night, on that long drive, was catatonic. After that reflexive braking, my limbs seemed to respond to Charles' directions without passing through central control. Had to, central control was out for the count. Numb.

By the time we got to the Halifax mansion, I had literally forgotten the carnage we left behind in Scotsburn, had forgotten that Pat and Suzanne had been left dead or dying on the cold hard ground. Cold, hard, and wet, for that biting wind had brought a freezing rain. And I had forgotten as well the two fugitives in the eaves of the barn, one surely dead by now—or just as good as.

I followed Charles past the stolid front doors of the Compton manor into the marble entry. I don't think he had a gun in hand any more. He didn't need one.

The old man waited for us in the solarium under an avacado tree. He nodded slightly to Charles behind me and I sensed rather than heard Charles leave the room.

"Sit down, Brigid," the old man said, smiling and charming as he had always been. "You must be exhausted. You've had quite a night."

Unprotesting, I sat in the chair his open gesture suggested.

The first hint I had of mental revival was the notion that Charles had killed the three of us, Suzanne, Pat and me, and that my Zombie-like trance was due to my having become one. It wasn't clear to me, however, whether I was Charles' Zombie, or if I belonged to the old man. I began to chuckle as I reflected on the trouble a Zombie could get into not knowing whom to obey.

I never saw the old man's command, nor had I been aware that Charles had returned. His slap, hard on the side of my head, caught me by surprise. The pain of the blow brought tears and, oddly, a sense of relief. Good thing it was the open palm of his hand, I thought, and not a gun, not like with Suzanne.

The pain of the blow was like something hard and firm to cling to, and I bit into it, sunk my nails into it. I wrapped my mind around the pain and it steadied me. Charles' hand, clean and manicured, appeared before my eyes holding a spotless, folded handkerchief. I took it and blew my nose.

When I could focus again, Old Man Compton was there smiling. He offered me cocoa, croissants, prosciutto, melon . "You must be hungry," he murmured sweetly.

I should have been. But I wasn't. I picked at the delicacies. In the background, I heard the canaries in their gilded cage and softly, from another room, another Bel Canto, Southerland and Horne, perhaps.

He waited until I had wiped my hands and laid down the

plate. Then he asked whether I wouldn't like to wash-up. I did, very much. It had been a long ride from Scotsburn. At the door of the washroom, Charles said, "Mrs. Donovan, don't try anything."

"Yeah," I said. And I didn't. What was to try?

A thoughtfully placed nailbrush cleaned the dried, caked blood from under my nails. Toothbrush, new, still in its plastic, coffin-shaped case. Brush and comb. In the mirror I saw a dull brown streak of blood on my forehead, where I had repeatedly pushed back my hair. My eyes were red like a drunk's. I didn't even try to clean the blood from my trousers where I'd wiped my hands after threatening Suzanne with the bloody butcher knife.

Back in the solarium, the old man and his doppelgänger had taken up their traditional pose, Charles hovering behind the wheelchair, a genie waiting. The old man's barely perceptible nod wafted him toward the open liquor cabinet where a silver tray with two thimble glasses had been set out, and "my" Kahlua alongside the Courvoisier.

Charles handed me the Kahlua silently, expectantly. Puzzled, I took it and looked to the old man to discover his intention.

"Won't you have some?" he asked mildly.

I shook my head and handed back the bottle.

Charles proffered the silver tray. I shook my head again.

"Take a glass," the old man urged, his voice silver like the tray. "You might change your mind."

It was easier to take it than to continue to refuse. I set the glass on the table before me.

Gingerly, Charles picked up the glass and returned the tray and the Kahlua to the cabinet top.

To me the old man said, smiling, "You are a tractable young woman, Brigid. I like that quality in women. Well now," he continued, "all we have to do is wait."

"Wait for what?" I asked.

"*Pace,*" he said. "*Pace.*" Italian as the sensuous curves of his lips.

In the background Southerland sang something by Mozart.

We passed the next hour, which was exceedingly long, in

silence. Toward the end of it the sky outside brightened, and Charles turned off the lights. The old man gave one of his little nods and Charles went out to return a few minutes later and announce, "No one answers."

"She must be on her way," the old man said. He asked whether I wanted anything.

"Yeah," I said. "I do. I want a few answers."

"Brigid," he said, "I suspect you know most of it. Why don't you start, and if you do have a question, why then I'll just fill in."

So I told him what I knew and what I suspected, but I said it flat out, like I knew it all.

"Your wife, Anna Maria Zuccollo, she went mad. Post-partem depression, maybe. It happened after the birth of your second child. And she never recovered. You had her put away, but you pretended she had died. You've been afraid that the madness was a family trait, and because you and she are cousins, you became afraid that your children would go mad, too. You didn't think they were sound enough for your dynasty."

I waited to hear his comments, but there weren't any. He just nodded, an invitation for me to continue.

"Did you know, when you married her, that you were cousins?" I asked.

His bright falcon eyes dimmed as if they had been hooded. From that memory, like a dream of the distant past, the old man read his history.

"We were already engaged when we found out," he said. "Our families had come at different times. Her mother, my aunt, had married a wop!" His delicate lips spat the ugly sound. "Zuccollo! How could we have guessed? She was pregnant. There was no going back. My friend, the priest who turned my schoolboy earnings into a real investment, he arranged it so we got a dispensation."

Then I understood. Having had a dispensation to marry in the first place, it would have been worse than awkward to try to have the marriage annulled. I wondered whether he had tried.

As if reading my thoughts, the old man said, "I didn't want an annulment." His bright eyes pierced again, "In this age of crass materialism, you may find it hard to believe, Brigid, but I was too much in love to marry anyone else."

"So you engaged in a 'morganatic' union with Pearl instead. Were there others?"

"Morganatic?" he said querulously. "Don't be absurd. Pearl and I were never married."

"I beg your pardon," I said.

"Most people," he continued when he'd recovered from his snit, "most people think Eddie was David...Arjuna's child."

"I'm not most people," I said.

"You might soon wish you were," he countered, meanly, the only mean words I had ever heard him say.

"Yeah," I agreed. "Maybe I already do. Tell me," I went on, "did you really think you could build your dynasty on Eddie and Julie? Did you really think you could keep the others—Arjuna, Paul, Suzanne—did you think you could keep them all in line? And what about Charles?" it suddenly occurred to me to ask. I raised my eyes to his stony face. "What orphan's child is he?"

The almost imperceptible nod, and Charles answered for himself. "Not family," he said, "but under a deeply felt obligation."

"Oh yeah?" I looked back to the old man for an explanation. He waved the matter away, "Nothing, really. Charles was born on the wrong side of someone else's blanket. But he's been like a son to me." He looked up into Charles' unsmiling face for confirmation. I wondered whether Charles was still buying the story.

"To answer your question, Brigid," the old man said, steepling his fingers in a Gothic arch, "each member of the family had a distinct place with much to gain. It was a stable structure. Pearl has an excellent head on her shoulders."

That he might have settled on Pearl to succeed him as lord of the manor didn't surprise me. Of them all, only Pearl had the calm hard-headedness to manage the empire the old man had constructed. But however excellent her head, I didn't think Pearl could stomach the massacre of her entire family and I said so.

"If it's Pearl your expecting," I hazarded, "maybe she stopped at Scotsburn on her way. I don't think she's going to like what she finds there."

"No," the old man conceded, "you're right. She doesn't like it. But she sees the necessity of it. And in the end, that's all that's important."

A gleam like mischief lit his eyes. "She doesn't much like my plan for you either. But..." He lifted his shoulders in a Gallic shrug.

"So tell me," I said, stunned still by grief and somewhat insouciant. "What *do* you have lined up for me?"

"Ah, a sad story of alcoholism and greed."

Alcoholism and greed? "Come again," I said.

"Yes, a relapse, fueled apparently by covetousness. Envy. Greed. Insatiable." With each word of this ridiculous indictment, his gnomish head swung mournfully from side to side. "So many witnesses to your envy, Brigid! Poor Sister Marie at St. Therese, she was quite shocked. You did tell her she could buy some pansy flats with the change from the money you extorted from her. A great deal of money. Did you do that?"

His horror was mock, his amusement genuine.

"Have I quit beating my wife, you mean." I said. Feeling was coming back, and it wasn't sorrow, but anger that I felt. I reflected on how from the beginning everyone, starting with Barney, had refused to pay me what had been promised, and how for the last six days I had been living mostly on plastic.

"What about this relapse?" I questioned. But I already knew.

"I have seen," the old man said, "others fall off their little AA pedestals. It is always quite painful. Suzanne will testify that you were obsessed with drink on the journey back from Smelt Brook, after you killed poor Mrs. MacDonald."

"Suzanne? You mean she's alive?" I looked inquiringly at Stone Face. He didn't even blink.

"Oh, she's alive," the old man assured me. "Sore jaw, but willing and able. She's a good girl, Suzanne is," he ended contentedly.

Then both those bullets, I realized, that Charles had so casually fired, had been aimed at Pat. Pain blazed hot in my chest and head. Dante had it wrong, beyond the ice comes the fire. I wanted to go back to being numb again. I looked over at the bottle of

Courvoisier. Never had I wanted anything so much in my life. I heard my voice saying, as if from a distance, "Suzanne's testimony might be construed as interested."

"Hers, yes," the old man nodded. He looked like a puppet to me suddenly, on strings; Charles, hovering over him, the puppeteer. His tinny old man's voice droned on. "But it will be harder to prove the self-interest of Charles here, or Donna. Donna served our dinner the other night. She saw you drink the wine and the Kahlua. And your prints are on the bottle and the glass there." He nodded at the delicate crystal witness sitting mute on the liquor cabinet, beside it the Kahlua bottle filled now, I was certain, with the real McCoy.

"So I'm a drunk and out for money. Tell me, why did I kill all those people?" But I didn't really care, and besides, I knew the answer. The ransom money. I remembered Suzanne's concern to get me away from Scotsburn, to have a look at the ransom, have me touch it, count it, get my fingerprints all over it. With lackluster triumph I announced, "I didn't touch the ransom. You'll never tie me to it."

"No," he conceded, "you didn't touch it. But you have touched a lot of other money these past few days. I believe when the authorities get their hands on the ransom, they will find that a lot of used bills have Brigid Donovan's fingerprints all over them. Quite a coincidence, wouldn't you say?"

The puppet's painted smile was complacent; the face of the puppeteer was still blank.

If survival is a state of mind, at that moment, my chances of getting through this were zero. Then, as I took in the case that had been laid brick by brick against me, in walked the master builder.

"Jacob," she said, "the rain held me up. Sorry, dear." She bent and kissed him.

It was Pearl. The old man was apparently right. Pearl's stomach was as hard as her head.

Chapter 21

"I think," Charles said, as he left me at the door to the room I had begun to regard as much my own as Suzanne's, "you will find everything you need. The exit has been blocked, so if you should want something, do remember the bell-pull."

I didn't bother to answer, and listened with indifference as he turned the key in the lock.

Pearl's greeting to me had been perfunctory. After "Hello, Brigid," she had turned to the old man and said, "There's no need of her now, Jacob." To me she said, "Get some rest, if you can. You'll need it."

The drapes in the bedroom were drawn, giving the room an aquatic atmosphere. On the edge of one island of furniture a standing lamp, like a washed-out sun, shed light on a bottle of Courvoisier, the very drink I had been longing for.

Tiredness, like an overweight bedfellow, had taken up my entire being. I would sit a moment, I thought. Take a sip of the brandy. I needed it.

And I was sure I could handle it. No problem. A small swallow, and then to bed.

Besides, what difference did it make. My fingerprints were all over the butcher knife at the Scotsburn murder scene. I was the last person to have seen Mrs. MacDonald alive.

And anyway, I was nothing but a drunk. That's all I had ever been, and all I ever would be.

So what difference did it make if I had a drink? None. None whatsoever.

I settled myself on the lounge and poured a sip of brandy into the thimble glass. If I didn't, somebody else would pour it for me, I reasoned. Why else had it been put there except as part of the frame-up. That same somebody, I realized, would spill brandy on my clothes, would soak me in brandy like a plum pudding waiting to be set on fire.

I paused, the delicate snifter not an inch from my lips. Might as well make it easy for them, I decided. In the bathroom was a pitcher and two real glasses. Tumblers. Much better. Better for me, easier for them. I'd pour myself a *glass* of brandy—fuck that small swallow! And fuck going right to bed. In fact, fuck everything!

The tumblers were where I had remembered them, invitingly placed on a small glass-topped table by the tub, or rather pool. Bundled on the hard tile floor of the Jacuzzi lay someone's body. Wisps of netting here and there gave her identity away. Someone had thoughtfully placed a pillow under Julie's head. Did that mean, I wondered, that she was still alive?

Garbled half thoughts shot through my head. Did they expect me to kill her for them too? Wasn't it enough to take the blame? Beside the tub lay the butcher knife that already bore my fingerprints. The blood on it had dried to an earthen brown.

I began to fumble with Julie's knots. My touch revived her. She had been tied and gagged, perhaps drugged, she seemed woozy at first, stretching and rubbing her wrists and ankles.

"Shit!" was the first word past those lovely lips. "What the fuck are you doing here? Did you tie me up?"

She rose and stepped out of the tub. I stood on the knife, hoping she wouldn't see it. She did.

"Don't worry. I'm not going to hurt you," she said, then added, "Not yet." She began to splash water on her face. "Where's Granddaddy? Do you know?"

For the next five minutes our conversation was Daliesque as she applied make-up at the three-way mirror and we spoke to each other's multiple images.

I asked about Arthur.

"Oh Arthur!" she said. Then in a mincy voice, "'How is Arthur? What did you do to Arthur?' All anyone ever thinks about is Arthur! Arthur is fine! Okay?"

" Yeah," I said. "I just wondered."

"He's asleep. What time is it?"

Lipstick carefully laid on lush lips.

"About seven o'clock," I said.

Lips carefully blotted, then, "He'll wake up soon."

"Oh."

"Now," she said, rising, her face splendidly restored, "To find Granddaddy."

"I wouldn't, if I were you," I cautioned.

"He's with Pearl, right?"

"Yeah."

"She won't get away with it."

Her insouciance staggered me. "*She* won't!" I said.

She looked at me sideways, through a cloud of blond hair that fell like a scrim over her ear, her eyes sly and watchful. "I thought you probably knew."

"I was worried about Arthur," I conceded. "But I don't know much."

Like a little girl, she needed to brag. "Well, someone had to stop Arjuna before he did something really stupid. I finally got Granddaddy to see that. No one else had the guts."

So long as Julie was talking to me, she wasn't out in the rest of the house. Since she had been left alive in the Jacuzzi, I figured whoever had left her there must have wanted her to go cannoning around. Tired of being manipulated, I decided it would be better to keep her where she was, in Suzanne's room. So long, that is, as I could do so safely.

"Arjuna was getting out of hand, was he?" I said, hoping I sounded sympathetic. Apparently I did, because Julie launched into a colorful explanation of what a "fuck-up" Arjuna had become.

"Do you know what he was gonna do?" she asked me, moving in close so I could smell her sour odor of alcohol and sleep. I had a fair idea, but I shook my head. She said indignantly, "He was gonna tell everyone my stigmata was a fake!"

She thrust her palms in my face. The scabs had hardened into calluses. The better to stab me with, I thought.

"Don't worry," she said, playfully jabbing my shoulder. Reading my thoughts. "I told you I wouldn't hurt you." Laughing, "Not yet, anyhow."

I said, "Yeah."

Then, "Did your Granddad suggest you try to pin the blame for killing Arjuna onto Pearl? Is that why you killed Arjuna that way? Like Pearl killed her own father?"

"Not exactly," Julie admitted. "Granddaddy is gonzo on that woman. But the way I figured it, if I got rid of Arjuna for him, and Pearl was found guilty—and someday she should have to pay for what she did, you know, when she was a girl and all, Gram said so, and Gram was right. So...." she shrugged. "With Pearl like gone, and Granddaddy seeing he could trust me to get things done and all...."

Her voice tailed off. I finished the sentence for her. "You would like take Pearl's place in your Granddad's hierarchy."

"Check! Hey, I've got to go find him."

"Wait!" I cried, catching a handful of cotton candy veils passing. "Tell me something."

Impatiently, she jerked herself free. "Watch it, Brigid!" And I caught, behind the pretty flowers, a glimpse of the panther, stalking.

"I was just going to have a brandy," I said. "Join me."

"A brandy! You?" she sneered. Then, amused, "Sure, why not? How long's it been?" she asked as I picked up the tumblers.

With my foot I edged the knife back behind the table. Out of sight, out of mind. "Oh, golly. In a while." I said.

"'Oh golly? Give me a break! Brigid!"

"Yeah. Maybe a drink will help."

"Couldn't hurt, that's for sure."

I gave her the lounge—which was a mistake—and took the armchair. I poured us each a glass of brandy.

"Here's mud in your eye," I said.

"Up yours," she said, civilly.

She seemed to enjoy her drink. She certainly enjoyed telling me her story. She enjoyed it so much that after protesting once, early on, she stopped noticing that I wasn't really drinking with her. I put the glass to my lips every once in a while, but the level of the brandy didn't fall. Once, pleading necessity, I took it with me to the john, and poured most of it out.

As I thought, the tidy family structure Old Man Compton had created—a place for everyone, and everyone in his place—had been overthrown by Julie's greed. But what had seemed a simple solution to her, had turned increasingly complicated.

"See," she said, "I knew if you came up here and all, you know, looking into Pearl's past, you'd find out about her killing her dad. I mean, like, I came across the story by accident, you know, in the Pictou library, last summer."

She said it had taken her a while to figure out how to put her startling discovery to use.

"Hey! I knew I was onto something, okay? But it took a while. Then I met Barney. You know, she doesn't like you much."

I told Julie this wasn't news and that the disregard was mutual.

"'The disregard'? You kill me. Have some more brandy. Hey, you've got a pretty good head for this stuff. I'm startin' to feel it."

"Practice," I said. "Like riding a bicycle. I guess you don't lose the knack."

"Yeah, I guess. I gotta find Granddad."

"Tell me about Barney," I suggested, pouring brandy into our glasses.

"Barney! She said you thought you were some wicked good detective. Like you thought you could solve anything. So I got to thinking. See Arjuna was, like, getting tired of being everyone's guru? Like restless? Like he just wanted to mess things up. You know, just for shit." She flashed me a smile. "Pearl says you figured out about the ransom notes."

I nodded. "I figured it out. But I'm not sure why you did it."

Julie smirked. "David really liked me. He was just tired of doing this guru business. Said he wanted to settle down." A mean look pinched her eyes. "He liked Arthur better, though. Anyway,

161

he didn't, like, want to leave me in the lurch. Granddad would never give me enough money to be independent, you know, like a lump sum. He's generous, but it's, like, you always have to ask. And do what he wants." The meanness overtook the sparkle in her eyes.

"So the ransom money was for you. To set you up. In business?"

"Yeah. With that money, and David's connections, you know, like in Asia? But what David didn't realize is I want what Pearl has, you know, like power."

I should have realized from the beginning that the envy and jealousy was Julie's for Pearl not the other way around. I had been blinded by Julie's youth and beauty, and the appearance of youthful innocence.

Julie needed to confide. "Anyway, I told Barney I thought Pearl wanted to kill me. But Barney didn't, like, believe me?" Julie sighed discontentedly and sank deeper into the softness of the couch. "After I got to know her better, I got the idea that Barney might, if she knew something bad about someone? She might, like, use it against them. To get what she wants. So I started hinting there was, like, somethin' goin' on between Arjuna and Pearl. You know, like I was havin' an affair with my own grandfather."

She giggled. "That's when Barney got interested. But she, like, still wasn't sure she believed me? She said, 'that's something Brigid could probably find out.' Barney doesn't like you much, you know," Julie said again as if the thought had just occured to her. "You probably don't know that—" Suddenly her eyes closed. The next sound was a watery snore. Spit in the corner of her mouth formed little bubbles. Julie no longer seemed fluffy and adorable.

Those first feelings of dislike and distrust she had roused in me that morning at the Cloisters returned. I should have paid better attention to my first reaction. Shouldn't have let myself be diverted by the kidnapping sideshow Arjuna staged before he died. Shouldn't have been distracted by the Compton carry-on. I'd been conned when I should have known better. First impressions are usually the best, better than staged ones at any rate.

So much about this case was show. The charity that masked

the shell game manipulation of money, inherited money, Church money. God knows whose money.

I recalled my first visit with Mrs. MacDonald in Smelt Brook. Her uneasiness over Julie's companion. She thought him odd, she said. She had meant Arthur, not Arjuna. Julie must have gone to land's end to wait for the ransom to be paid. But the old woman, the friendly great-grandmother, said no.

She must have refused to let Julie and Arthur stay. I wondered how forcefully she had recommended they cleanse their conscience. Had she said she would call the Mounties if Julie wouldn't? Said this as she calmly rocked, looking out to sea?

What I didn't know would fill a tome. And I wanted to know. Wanted desperately, before I died, to know the truth. Be able to say the truth. And, despite my foolishness along the way, I wanted at the end to be like those MacDonald women. I believed that Faith and Hope, like their mother, had finally stood up to Julie, and for that, they had paid with their lives.

I also wanted to understand. And I wanted a glimpse into the mind of this cotton candy psychopath, Julie, who littered bodies the way some people litter tissues. Maybe, I realized, I didn't have far to look. Julie hadn't created mayhem for any reasons I could understand. She seemed to have murdered casually. Like the little tailor swatting flies. Like thousands of Iraqi soldiers buried alive in the slaughter called Desert Storm.

I wondered how many Iraqis had had to die so I could afford, when the mercury hit ten below, to let my engine run while I picked up some things in the Seven-Eleven. Our priorities were different, Julie's and mine, but the greed was the same. She at least did the dirty work herself.

I thought for one mad moment of myself as an insect about to be squashed in Julie's random swatting. In India they wear gauze, protecting small insects from a sticky death. Insects like those black flies I murder by the dozen every day in spring because they annoy me. The thought made me earnest not to annoy Julie. I shook her—but gently. "Julie, come on! Wake up! What don't I know? Be a sport, Julie."

But her sweet pouty lips were pursed in slumber, little bubbles of spit, was all they emitted.

Julie said she had hinted to Barney that Pearl and Arjuna had once been lovers and she had let Barney think Arjuna was her grandfather. I remembered the way Pearl had looked at Arjuna's picture the morning after he was killed. I had thought at the time the look was fond. I had believed Julie when she said Pearl was jealous of her. I had believed that Arjuna was Eddie's father, that Eddie was the illegitimate offspring of a servant girl and scion. To be fair, maybe Julie had thought so, too. I needed to know whether she knew Old Man Compton was Eddie's father.

Carefully I shook her again. She woke. It took her a moment to focus.

"Whassup?" she muttered.

"You were telling me about Barney," I said. "She did think you were in danger. So did Pat."

"Yeah, maybe," said the pretty lips, uninterested. Julie patted her bedraggled finery. "Barney doesn't care shit about that. It was like, you know, window dressing. Barney's into blackmail. That's why I told her Arjuna was my granddaddy. Barney wanted evidence she could use to force Eddie... Thas my daddy."

Julie sneezed. The spray hit me full in the face. She found it amusing. I thought of all the little flies I had squashed while they ate supper and managed to restrain myself. "Yes?" I said mildly.

"Barney wanted Eddie and Arjuna outta Surry. She had this other scam goin' with some nun, I forgetter name."

Julie yawned and rubbed her eyes. She fumbled for a cushion. I didn't want to lose her yet, I wanted to hear the rest of her story. Wanted to know how much of what I suspected was true. How wicked good I was as a detective. If I were going to die soon, I wanted to have that satisfaction.

I bent over her. Her breath was a mixture of sour alcohol, half digested, and fresh Courvoisier. I said, "You're not talking about Barney and that silly Santa Clara?"

She perked up. "Yeah. Santa Clara. You're not as dumb as you look. You know her?"

I did, but not the way I once had hoped to. Not in the Biblical sense. I just nodded.

"You know she's supposed to heal people. Barney wanted to set up a scam with her, in Surry. She didn't, like, want the competition from me and Arjuna."

This is what Suzanne had told me. I was inclined to believe it. It explained Barney's eagerness to have me 'investigate' Pearl. She wanted information she could use to run Arjuna and Julie out of town.

Julie's face had slackened. Her lips had lost the tautness that gave them beauty. She said, giggling sloppily, "So I told Barney I thought that maybe Arjuna was my granddaddy!"

She started to hiccough. The last time I heard her hiccough she had been weeping. It was the morning Arjuna died. Died in a fire she had set after carefully tying him to his bed. Ignorant, I'd felt pity then. Now I felt disgust. It must have shown on my face.

"So what the fuck's wrong with you? You thought we were screwing, too!"

"Actually," I said, "I thought Arjuna wanted people to think so, but that it wasn't true. You weren't having an affair with him. And he wasn't your grandfather. Your father, Eddie, wasn't Arjuna's son. He was Jacob Compton's. Arjuna wasn't your grandfather. Old Jacob Compton is."

"Well geewhiz! Go to the head of the class." Suddenly she looked sly. "But Barney fell for it. She wanted to believe it. And she wanted you to find the evidence. So that Dad and Arjuna wouldn't get their precious temple. So she and Saint whatsername could do their thing. She sure got you hooked."

Julie giggled. She belched. She said, "I knew it wouldn't take a rocket scientist to find out how great-granddaddy MacDonald died. So! Once you agreed to help, I burned up the yogi!" She laughed delightedly. "Once you found the story of great-grand-dad's murder, Pearl'd be blamed for killing Arjuna."

It was my arrogance, then, that was responsible for Arjuna's death. "Don't worry about it," said Julie, reading my thoughts again. "I hadda nother plan if you didin wanna invess...you know, Pearl for me. Christ I'm tired."

"Pearl must not have thought I would find out anything," I said. "Or she wouldn't have sent me to Nova Scotia."

"Bull shit!" said Julie. "She sent you to Nova Scotia so Suzanne could keep her eye on you. Poor Brigid, Ace detective!" She sniggered.

"Anyway!" Julie flounced a little. "I Xeroxed the story. I would have sent it to you if you hadn't discovered it for yourself." She waggled her finger at me. "Sorry, Brigid. But you were going to discover that story come hell or,"—hiccough— "high water."

"What's in it for you?" I asked.

"Granddaddy needs me." She smiled sweetly, the picture of innocence, albeit innocence a little disheveled.

Afraid to go too far, I hesitated over my next question. The silence between us grew and Julie became restless.

"Granddaddy would give you anything you want." I said it as a statement of fact. She responded with a shrill laugh.

"What I wanted was for him to die. Once I'd made my arrangements."

"Why? What was it you couldn't have had for the asking?" But I knew, and I said it. My voice must have echoed with my incredulity. "Was it...the power?"

She looked at me scornfully. "When did you miss having an allowance?"

Always, I thought. Always. The vow of poverty had always attracted me: obey these rules, and forget about the rest; we'll take care of you. But I could see the Compton off-spring had been brought up to different aspirations. Some of them at least.

"You're lucky, you know, I like you," she said. "'Cause Pearl, she has a plan for you you won't like at all. Not one little bit. We gotta take care a Pearl." She struggled to sit upright.

Cautiously, I restrained her. "What do you mean?" I asked.

"Pearl wansa kill me. That wasn't true before, but it sure as hell is now. Kill me and blame you. Thas why she brought me here."

"Why aren't I surprised."

"Don't worry. Granddaddy won't let 'er."

"Oh, no? Good."

She leered up at me. "But you're in deep shit. You know that?"

"I guessed as much. They intend to frame me for the murders

of Mrs. MacDonald and Faith and Hope. "Julie, why did you have to kill them?"

"Oh, them," she said and yawned. She knuckled her eyes unconcerned as a child.

"Yeah," I said, "them. Why did you kill them?"

She snorted. "They said I had to give myself up. Me! I had to give myself up, and all the time it was 'Poor Arthur this' and 'Poor Arthur that.' The little shit."

She was genuinely aggrieved: At the injustice done *her*.

"Gram said I couldn't stay with her. You know, until I got the ransom? Like I was planning to stay there in Smelts Brook while everyone was lookin' for us. After they found out Arthur'd kidnapped me." She laughed. "Arthur!" She said his name with contempt.

"What about Arthur," I said. "What did you plan to do with him? Kill him, too?"

"Why not," she said. "He'd be better off dead. God, he is such a jerk. You know, Gram liked him?" Julie shook her head in disbelief. "Unbelievable. Told me to take care of him. Get this, she said she made a mistake with Pearl; never gave her a chance to get square with God. And she wasn't gonna make the same mistake with me. She said we could turn ourselves in, you know, the next day in Pictou. She said we could have a day just to get ourselves ready. So what else could I do?" She shrugged.

"Did Faith and Hope threaten to turn you in?"

"Yeah." Julie was bored. But she continued after a pause during which she examined her nails, holding them up to her eyes, looking perhaps for her reflection. Mirror, mirror. "After you came, they got kinda nervous. Said you knew we were there. Did you see our light? I told Arthur not to leave it on. He is such a weirdo. Do you believe it? He's scared of the dark!"

"I saw it," I said. "But at the time, I thought it might be the moon—reflecting off the window up there. I wasn't sure."

"Yeah, well Faith says, 'Brigid's gonna send the Mounties!' Dum de dum dum! Big deal. She said, 'You gotta turn yourself in tomorrow, Julia.' I said bull shit."

She suddenly stood up.

Startled—no—scared shitless, I fell back and my chair toppled over. She stood over me, stood astride me, and laughed.

"God, Brigid. You are such a jerk! Where's that knife?"

I promised the god of black flies to mend my ways, wear gauze over my mouth in future. Not even think about killing one of them. "Julie," I stammered.

She slapped her knee and threw back her head, the laughter shaking her slight frame. When she calmed down, she said, still choking a little on her mirth, "Get up, Brigid. You look ridiculous. We need to get outta here. Or we're history."

I got to my feet in stages, afraid to turn my back on her. When I was upright I said, tentatively, "Um, the door is locked, remember?"

"I figured. We can get out through the window. If you don't mind a little jump. It's easy."

"If it's easy," I said, "then count on it: That's what they're waiting for us to do."

"Yeah. You're right. I thought of that, too. But then I forgot. Shouldn't have drunk all that fucking brandy. Jesus, but I need some sleep. I hada plan. What in Christ's name was it?"

She pursed her lips, or tried to. I could feel the alcohol mushing her brain. Empathy. Mine had been mushed a few zillion times before. I wondered whether she was young enough to clear her head and remember what it was she had planned.

She started to giggle, suddenly energized. "I remember! Right! Fire. Don't worry," she said, apparently tickled by my expression, "I'm not gonna tie you to the bed. I told you. I like you, Brigid."

Then, as an afterthought, "Even if you are a goddamned jerk most of the time. Bring me those candles over there. And look for some paper. We're gonna have us a little fire here in Suzy's room."

Chapter 22

And a little bonfire is what we had. But big enough to set off the sprinklers and fire alarm. After barricading the door, Julie and I stationed ourselves on either side of the escape route, a window overlooking the topiary zoo. Beside the giraffe's leg stood a thuggish looking fellow with brooding muscles and a sunny disposition, whistling "Danny Boy" until he heard the fire alarm go off.

"When he splits," Julie instructed, "that's when we get out of here."

"How do you know he'll split?"

"Bubba? He's so dumb his brain rattles. When the bells start ringing he'll think his mother's calling him to supper. What you wanna do is grab hold of Griffy's head and kinda swing down."

"Griffy?"

"The giraffe, Brigid! The giraffe."

"Oh right."

"Watch me."

"Yeah, okay. What then? Once we're down?"

But Julie was already half out the window. From the hall I could hear a massive assault begin against our barricaded door.

I leaned out and grabbed Griffy by his horns, just like Julie. But I didn't swing free and drop nimbly, as she had. My hands, cut by newly clipped twigs, slipped and I fell awkwardly, my breath knocked out of me.

For a long time all I could deal with was the bonfire in my

chest and needing to breath. I forgot about Julie, and I forgot about running away. I didn't hear the footsteps cross the grass, or the whoosh of the sap slicing the air above me. One minute I was struggling to breathe and the next I was struggling to regain consciousness.

Odd how slowly our brain assembles unfamiliar information, how clumsily the different pieces are turned this way and that, like a difficult jigsaw, to see where they fit together to create a pattern, form a picture. My jigsaw, as I regained consciousness, seemed to have only one characteristic Blackness. Complete and uniform. The only bump in the monotony of nothingness was a beat, regular as a metronome, in my head, pounding like a hammer pounds a forge. I hurt. I. Corner piece. Starting point. I hurt therefore I am. Cartesian dualism overcome. I longed to be rid of a brain that could have a thought like that at a time like this, and could hurt so much besides.

I could move. I wasn't tied. But the space was small, and I seemed to be curled in a corner. It smelled familiar, like home, like childhood. Lemon oil. Lemon oil and dust. I began to grope. But carefully, carefully.

The soft curls of the dust mop startled me, so like a head of hair. But the standing straws I recognized at once: Broom. So, someone had dumped me in a broom closet. Knocked me out and dumped me. But before that I had fallen. It all came back suddenly then, like the blow that had winded me. Pat was dead. Charles had shot her. Shot her twice.

I mistook the layers of Julie's netting for a pile of dirty dust rags. Until the pile began to move and make slight noises like mice squeaking.

She had been tied and a rag stuffed in her mouth. It was hard, in the dark, to locate the knots, and impossible to untie them. As I tried unsuccessfully to loosen her bonds, Julie's wriggling became more violent. And her squeaks. I figured she wanted the gag removed. I would have. But I just couldn't bear the thought of listening to her. Not with my headache. Not in the tight confines of that closet.

Gingerly I stood up and began to feel around. It must be some tight fitting door, I thought, not to let in any light. I found the knob and turned it, the door opened. But still no light to speak of. It was a moment before I realized that night had fallen. That some twelve hours had elapsed since my fall from the window. Julie thumped the floor behind me.

"Take care," I said, closing the broom closet.

I took my bearings. Several doors converged on the hall where I stood. One of them led up to Suzanne's room. No point in going through that one. One led outside. I gently massaged the back of my head. A goose had nested there and laid an egg. I decided not to hazard it having twins. That left the door into the kitchen and the rest of the house. I opened it.

Darkness again. I decided to risk a light, better than blundering through the dark looking for a door, bumping into God knows what. The switch was in the hallway, so it took a while to find it.

The kitchen might have been in a restaurant, so large and well equipped it was. For a giddy moment I wondered whether I was, after all, still in the Compton mansion. The door into the house was past a range big enough for a school of chefs to play at. Beside it, cumbersome as an iceberg, hulked a double doored refrigerator.

I couldn't resist taking a look inside the box. Forlornly centered were an egg carton, a cardboard container of 1% milk, a jar of strawberry jam, and a tub of Mrs. Filbert's, the cover half off. Just like my house. I wondered where the old man kept the delicacies he offered rabbits like me for bait. Maybe he just had Charles call a local deli. Suzanne's folks, Paul and Lucy, they must have their own kitchen I thought. I wondered where the two of them had been that morning during the hullabaloo.

Moving around in fresh air had done wonders for my head. The pain had subsided to a dull ache. Before committing myself to the world beyond the kitchen, I took a moment to remind my Guardian Angel of her responsibilities regarding my health and well-being.

Wall sconces, like the ones in the upstairs hallway, lighted the long passage beyond the kitchen. I heard a murmur of voices coming from the Versailles room. It must be an affair of state. Hope for a moment stirred the sodden mass of my despair, and I realized how without hope I had been. But hope quickly succumbed to memory. The memory of two shots, the shots that killed Pat. Killed Pat and my own interest in living. Just as well. Hope is a poor companion for danger.

I moved cautiously down the hall. I could probably have run, the carpet was thick enough to absorb any sound, the crash of dishes, the sound of weeping.

The Versailles room doors, ornately carved with gospel scenes, stood open. Inside all was splendor. Three crystal chandeliers spilled dazzling light on a setting Titian might have painted. The central figure was dressed in a cardinal red gown. He wore a funny cap on his head, like a yamulka. He looked for all the world like a real live Cardinal, and after a while I realized that that is what he really was.

A quarrel was in progress, an unfamiliar voice saying, "Your Eminence, it is clear that only the strongest measures—"

Charles interrupted. "Your Eminence, there's been enough..."

"But your Eminence, this frame-up, it is out of the question. It never will hold up," the stranger asserted. "And Giulia, surely your Eminence sees—"

"I'll take care of Julie." The voice was high and dry, an old man's voice. Jacob Compton's voice, but broken.

"Surely, your Eminence, you can see the girl cannot be trusted...."

"Karl?" his Eminence said. "Tell me, your view is?"

Charles began, "Your Eminence, the bloodshed has been unfortunate, however..."

That's when I walked in.

"However, what?" I said.

The silence, for a moment, was complete. Foretaste of the grave, the obscene thought flashed my mind.

"Who are you?" asked the man in the pretty red dress.

"I'm Brigid Donovan. Only a little of my blood's been shed. However—"

Charles' voice overrode my own. "This is the meddling woman I told you about, your Eminence."

"The detective," his Eminence, in a brittle voice, said, not quite making the "th." "Se detektif," is how it sounded.

Hearing the accent, I thought I finally understood. Understood what Julie had never suspected—that the Compton fortune was less personal than institutional. That it really wasn't Granddaddy's to dispose of as he would. But Pearl, I was sure, had known. This, perhaps, was what lay at the bottom of her difficulties with Julie.

"Yeah," I said to the man in red. "I'm the detective. And this thug," I jerked my thumb at Charles, "murdered my best friend, a nun, as a matter of fact. Though you probably wouldn't approve of her convent. You are the Grand Inquisitor, aren't you? Cardinal, whatsit, Maussinger?"

"Brigid, Brigid," murmured the old man. I hadn't noticed him, in his wheelchair, curled like a desiccated leaf, remnant of a by-gone season. "Have some respect for his Eminence, for his office."

"Fuck his office," I lashed out. "And fuck his Eminence. What's wrong, Jacob? Did Julie make them nervous? I guess she didn't know she had to get permission to commit murder." I turned on Charles. "But you did get approval...for killing Pat? Before hand I mean."

Charles stepped from behind the wheelchair and started toward me. I drew back a step, turned toward the Cardinal and said, "Jacob Compton is nothing but a front to launder money for the Vatican. The orphanages, the homeless shelters, all those fancy foundation deals. They're fronts. How many shelters does it take to clean money made in a brothel?" I asked his Eminence, as if I really wanted to know, imagining shopping bags of bills, deposited daily as charitable donations.

Then I asked the sixty-four dollar question: "When did you start to get nervous about this weird family you had fronting for you in North America?"

Charles took my elbow. "That's enough," he said.

"You going to do it right here?" I challenged. "In front of his Eminence?" I snickered.

"Make zis voman be quiet!" ordered the Cardinal.

I turned to the stranger in the room. Elegant as a ne'er-do

well, about forty, blow-dry hair but Valentino side-burns neatly flecked with gray, slim silk suit and shiny shoes. Too pretty to be anything but a banker. A Vatican banker, as necessary for the salvation of souls as the seven sacraments. I wondered whether they were specially ordained, or only specially promoted.

"Who are you?" I asked. "A monsignor? Monsignor Zuccollo, perhaps?" His look of disdain for me and for my question suggested I was off the mark.

Maybe then he was some Pope's 'nephew.' The Banco D'Ambrosiano was formally secular—and formidably corrupt. Tied to the Vatican, Banco D'Ambrosiano had scandalized even the irreligious during the eighties. There was a persistent rumor that the short-lived Pope who succeeded Pope John XXIII was murdered because he had tried not to contain the scandals, but, cure the corruption.

"You're just an ordinary banker then," I charged. "Not that anyone would call Banco D'Ambrosiano an ordinary bank."

He sniffed. I'd got it right this time. Banco D'Ambrosiano, bank of the Vatican, its octopus arms embracing the world, its holdings a dense mystery, protected now and then by death, like the alleged suicide hung under a London bridge some years ago.

"And who the hell are you, Charles?" I asked next.

Charles, smirking, said, "It is I who am the Monsignor. Personal assistant to the Cardinal. Until our good friend, Mr. Compton, needed an assistant. In some return for his devotion over a lifetime…"

"Devotion!" I snorted, turning on the old man. "What are you, Jacob?" I challenged, "the Canadian Grand Dragon of Opus Dei?" This was no time to debate theology, but the organization Opus Dei, in my opinion, was thinly veiled fascism, born and bred in Spain under Franco. My own sympathies lay with liberation theology and its concern for the oppressed. Why root for the winning team? Jesus didn't.

"Opus Dei? Opus Dei?" said the old man querulously. "They went soft. Years ago. God called me. We have supplanted Opus Dei. Everywhere. Communion and Liberation!" He made neat little crosses with his thumb, in the furrows of his brow, across the fine bow of his mouth, on his wizened breast.

"Communion and Liberation?" I echoed. "What's that?"

Charles said, cuing from the Cardinal's nod, "The Church's bulwark against Satan."

"Satan!" I scoffed, "As in the 'preferential option for the poor'?"

There I was in his Eminence's face, quoting Liberation Theology at him.

"Satan like Sandinistas maybe? Was Ollie North into you for money to support the Contras?" I taunted. "Now that Franco's dead, do you decide which tyrannies to bankroll?"

I wheeled on the dapper banker. "Or is it Satan as in threatened profits? What's good for Banco D'Ambrosiano is good for your immortal soul? Never mind what cesspool the profits came from?"

The Mastroiani look-alike pulled a silk kerchief from his breast pocket, placed it against his nose. He looked up at me, his eyes clearly pained by what he saw.

I jerked my elbow free from Charles and turned on him. "What happened? Did the old man get out of hand? His dynastic problems, did they upset your calculations? Were you afraid of the scandal? Is that why they made you into his keeper?"

"Make zis voman be quiet," commanded his Eminence.

"Tell me, Eminence." I crouched, my head level with his own. "When did you decide to step in? Was it when the heir apparent turned Buddhist?"

The Cardinal looked bored.

"No," I said. "Arjuna's antics were okay so long as they made money. It was Jacob Compton's unreliability that alarmed you, wasn't it? His needing to protect his family from scandal. Tell me, what have you planned for Julie?" I asked. "For Julie and for me?"

The old man stirred in his chair, leaned forward, his wasted body strained, a prisoner waiting to hear his sentence read. He knew no more than I did. Our fates, I realized, hadn't been decided. That was the argument I had walked in on.

The Cardinal's hand, bright with amethyst and gold, slapped the arm of his chair. "Someone shut zis voman up."

The languid banker looked toward Charles, who said, half-heartedly, "Mrs. Donovan, please...."

"You didn't think it would work, the old man's hare-brained scheme to frame me and let Julie go," I told the Grand Inquisitor. "So what have you decided?" I asked. "Kill the two of us? Hang us under MacDonald Bridge? Or knife us and dump us with the other bodies in Scotsburn. You going to blame it all on Arthur? But what about the old man? What do you plan to do with him? Or don't you think that's important. Maybe he'll die of a broken heart."

I looked at old Jacob Compton. His head lay inert now against the mean blue vinyl of the wheelchair, his eyes closed, his heart already broken. In the Cardinal's silence, he had discerned his fate. His fate and Julie's.

His Eminence clapped his hands once, sharply, the sound brutal as flint striking flint. A spark to light a conflagration. He addressed me for the first time directly. "Zees are spiritual matters you know nosing about."

"Murder is not spiritual, you son of a bitch!" I said.

His Eminence enjoined the company once more, "Make zis voman be quiet!"

"Brigid, it's okay," a familiar voice behind me said. It sounded just like Pat and took my breath away. I turned and there she was. With Suzanne. And another familiar face. Jason, my favorite Mountie. From Smelts Brook, the one who'd read me my rights five days before. Five days that seemed a lifetime.

"Hi, Granddad!"

Suzanne's greeting seemed to revive the old man. She squeezed my elbow as she passed on her way to him. But I didn't pay much attention. My eyes and Pat's were locked on a channel they couldn't get off, not mine, not hers.

"Who are your friends, Suzanne?" The old man's conventional inquiry, in the circumstances, was startling. Jason answered.

"Mr. Compton? I'm Jason MacKenzie. Royal Canadian Mounted Police out of Cape Breton. Suzanne Compton," he inclined his head toward Suzanne, "your granddaughter, I believe, reported your life to be in danger. She asked me to accompany her here."

"You've no jurisdiction," Charles began.

"That's not quite clear," returned the Mountie. "I am the officer in charge of a murder committed in Smelt Brook. Our investigations require us to question a woman we have been informed is being detained here."

A slight flicker of his eyelid was the first indication that Jason MacKenzie had noticed my presence.

Charles took charge for the Vatican crew. "That's the woman," he said, indicating yours truly. "If she was detained, it was in our collective self-defense."

"Yes?" said Jason dryly.

"Well," Charles bluffed, "you have some idea, apparently, that she is, uh, dangerous."

"I see," said Jason MacKenzie in a neutral voice.

"You'll find the evidence upstairs."

"I see," Jason said again.

His Eminence broke in on this tête á-tête to say, "Vould someone get rid of zis man."

Suzanne began to laugh. "Vould someone get rid of all zeese men!"

For the first time I really looked at her. She had, I saw, changed her clothes since I last had seen her. She didn't look at all like tenure anymore. She wore the same harem pants I'd seen on the beach at Inverness and her hair was wild as a belly dancer's. I sensed it wasn't only her hair she had liberated.

The old man seemed to notice for the first time, too. "Suzanne! What a way to dress," he chided. "What will his Eminence think? Go change!" he ordered. Revived and domineering as ever.

"Granddaddy! Never mind about him," said Suzanne. "We've come to get you."

"Shush, child!" he urged. "It's his Eminence. Come to visit."

"Grandfather, they don't need you anymore. Don't you understand? You're going to end up sharing a room with Grandmother. Or dead. Trust me." She stooped and kissed his cheek. "Where's Pearl?"

Charles answered. "Miss Compton, you would be wise to do

as your grandfather has suggested. Dr. MacDonald has retired so that your grandfather and his Eminence can conclude their business."

"Conclude their business?" Suzanne's eyebrows curled over her fine almond eyes.

"Monkey business!" I intervened. "They intended to blame me for the murders." I turned to Jason MacKenzie. "That's the evidence Big Boy here wants to show you. They've got the knife. And it does have my prints on it. But I can explain that."

Charles smirked at the Mountie. I started to get defensive. Suzanne stopped me. She said, "Mr. MacKenzie, perhaps it would be best if you took my grandfather and Mrs. Donovan downtown for questioning?" She added, "Liked we talked about?"

"Not Mr. Compton," said Charles, taking hold of the handle of the old man's chair.

The sudden motion startled Jacob Compton. Alarm flared in his eyes. He reached out a claw to Suzanne. "Suzanne, I do want to go with you."

She took his hand in both of hers. "You bet," she said.

"Zis iss intolerable," said the man in red. "Karl! Do somesing."

"No. Don't do anything! Any of you! Don't even breathe."

In the doorway stood Pearl. Behind her stood Julie. Between them I sensed, rather than saw, a bloodstained butcher knife pointing into Pearl's back.

Chapter 23

"Charles," Julie said, "get the Mountie's gun and give it here to me."

"Zis iss terrible," said the man in the yamulka. "Karl, bring zis Mountie's gun now to me."

"You do that, Charles, and you can kiss Grandma here goodbye," threatened Julie.

"For God's sake, Charles, do what she says." The old man's voice croaked like a frog's. A little frog.

Julie laughed. The sound was harsh. Not diaphanous at all. She said into Pearl's ear, her voice an evil whisper, "What did I tell you, Grandma! I told you Granddaddy wouldn't let anything happen to you!"

Commandingly then, Julie barked, "Charles! You have two seconds."

"Karl!" The Grand Inquisitor menaced.

"Charles, please do what she says," pleaded the old man.

"I think, your Eminence," said Charles, "Julie means what she says."

"Damn straight," said Julie.

"Zis is outrageous, young woman!" fumed the Cardinal.

Charles advanced on the Mountie. "Raise your hands slowly, away from the holster." Gingerly, Charles pulled out the revolver.

"Bring it here. There that's good," said Julie. "Careful. Lay it on the ground. Now back off."

You could almost hear Julie's brain working. She should have told Pearl to pick up the gun. In the end, though, Julie couldn't bear to let her grandmother even touch the weapon. First, Julie toed the pistol back to an inch or so from her left foot. Then she said, "Don't even think about it, Grannie."

Quickly, Julie dropped Pearl's arm and stooped for the gun. It took less than a second, but it was time enough. Pearl threw herself to the right. Jason MacKenzie dove over her, tackling Julie.

Blood like a fountain rose in the air and fell.

Pat, who was closest, leaped onto the pile. Charles turned, then he too threw himself into the stew.

What the hell! I decided and dove in.

Everything was sticky in there. Blood, I guessed. What I wanted was the gun. What I didn't want was the knife.

In the end the knife got me. Got most of us. Got Julie bad. Really bad. Later they said it was an accident. Who knows. Maybe it was. Or maybe Julie's premonition was right. Maybe Julie really did know that Pearl, one day, would kill her. Pearl, an organization man if ever a woman was.

Somehow it was I who ended up holding the gun. I decided the person to aim it at was the guy in red silk. The others, all except Julie, slowly got to their feet. Pearl's arm was bleeding bad. Most of the blood had spurted over Jason. He told Pat to take care of Pearl and he told me to hand over his revolver. I was glad to.

Suzanne called 911.

The ambulance crew, when they got there, had their hands full. Julie was dead. So was old Mr. Compton. Heart attack apparently. One of the EMTs called the Halifax police.

Jason, Pat, Charles and I had our nicks cleaned and bandaged. Pearl refused to be taken to the hospital. She asked for a butterfly bandage, said that would do nicely. When the nice young man with the bandages was done with her, Pearl went to the old man's side.

At first we thought he had fallen asleep. He hadn't. Not so he'd ever wake up again, anyhow. Pearl decided then that she would, after all, go with the ambulance. But first, she asked his Eminence to bless the bodies. Some blessing.

The bodies blessed and ready to be removed, Charles said to the Halifax police captain, who had arrived in the middle of the Cardinal's ceremony, "His Eminence has a plane to catch."

Captain Harkey was a Clark Kent look alike. But in manner he was Caspar Milquetoast. Bowing and scraping, he said, "Of course. Of course. Your Eminence." His head bobbed up and down like a bashful schoolboy's. To Pearl, before she left, he said, with deference, "How would you like this handled, Mrs. MacDonald?"

"Call me in the morning, Stuart."

"Certainly," he said.

When the carved doors closed behind the parade of people, both alive and dead, Suzanne raised her hand, fingers curled over palm, and called out, "Ciao bene."

For a moment we were silent, the four of us who were left, Suzanne, Pat and me—us and Jason MacKenzie of the Royal Canadian Mounted Police. Then Suzanne added, "The King is dead. Long live the Queen."

"Amen," I said. "So, tell me. What happened?"

What happened is: First of all, obviously, Charles had not killed Pat.

"How could he have missed?" I asked. "It was almost point blank range."

Suzanne shook her head. "He didn't miss. Bad as they are, that Vatican crew, they don't kill people. Usually," she amended. "Charles just wanted...," Suzanne faltered. "He wanted," she said finally, in a rush, "to break your spirit. I'd told him..."

"That I was fond of her?" My disgust of Suzanne, of all the Comptons, warred with my pity.

I decided to be mad at the Vatican for a while. "You say they don't kill people usually. But they considered framing me for what Julie had done."

"Well, that's different," Suzanne said, and you could see she really thought it was.

"Different for you, maybe," I muttered. Turning to the Mountie, I asked, "How's your cousin Helen?" He assured me Helen was fine. "How did you get involved?" I asked. "I mean, down here in Halifax and all."

"You can thank your friend here for that," said Jason, with a light nod of his head toward Suzanne.

Suzanne, happy to be on more favorable ground, was eager to explain. "I remembered your saying that the RCMPs on Cape Breton aren't under Grandfather's thumb like they are around Halifax. I phoned him."

"It took you long enough to get here," I crabbed. Ungrateful.

"You tell her," Suzanne said, turning to Pat.

Pat took up the story. Charles' blow had winded her, but hadn't knocked her out. As soon as Charles and I had driven off, Julie and Arthur emerged from the barn. Arthur, meek as a mendicant, obeyed Julie's instructions to tie up the two helpless women, one unconscious, the other unable to breathe. Suzanne came to in the middle of it all. She tried to convince Julie that if no one else were killed, the family planned to have me, Brigid Donovan, framed for the murders already committed. But that wouldn't happen, said Suzanne, if Julie killed anyone else. Suzanne especially.

"You knew?" I asked. "That they were planning to kill me?"

Suzanne blushed. "I tried to help," she said, shifty-eyed.

"Oh sure you tried to help. My Aunt Fanny you tried to help! What you tried to help was yourself to the Compton inheritance. You're as bad as Julie!"

"That's not fair!" she declared. "I sent you to St. Elizabeth's alone. So you could find out the truth."

"Bull shit! You were herding me. And you knew where I was headed."

At that point, grudgingly, Pat pointed out that it had been Suzanne who insisted they call Jason MacKenzie to the rescue.

I let it go. In my heart I had to acknowledge my share of responsibility for the plot against me. I certainly hadn't made it difficult for Suzanne to set me up. "Get a life!" the woman at the meeting had said. Did she mean by that to get a rich honey? I didn't think so.

"How did you get free?" I asked.

"Pearl. She came, oh, maybe half an hour later," Pat said.

"I'm surprised Julie didn't kill her, too."

Julie hadn't had a chance. Pearl had come on the scene quietly while Julie and Suzanne were yelling. Pearl had a gun. She slammed it against the side of Julie's head. Arthur, bewildered, followed Pearl's instructions to untie Pat and Suzanne. He balked, however, at tying up his sister.

"What did Pearl do about that?" I asked.

Suzanne snorted. "What do you think she did. She knocked him out."

"Just like that?"

"Just like that."

"She told him to tie his shoe," Pat explained. "When he bent over..."

With Julie and Arthur taken care of, Pat, Pearl and Suzanne had consulted. Suzanne convinced Pearl that framing me was no solution to their problem. It hadn't been hard. "Pearl knew for a long time that Julie was a disaster waiting to happen," said Suzanne. "But Grandfather wouldn't hear of scandal touching any of us. Pearl said she would see what she could do. She took Julie and left us with Arthur. That's when we thought of getting Officer MacKenzie to help."

Pat took my arm, then, and said, "I'd like to get out of here."

I said, "Fine with me," and looked inquiringly at the Mountie.

"You're free to go, Mrs., uh, Donovan. We know how to get in touch, should it prove necessary. It seems clear to me that Mrs. MacDonald was murdered by her great granddaughter. And that is the only case in my jurisdiction."

He smiled. I wondered whether he liked me. After all. "Say hello to Helen for me," I said.

"I'll be sure to do that. Good-bye Miss." He nodded to Pat.

"Wait, I'll come with you," said Suzanne.

"No."

That's all Pat said. But Suzanne knew 'Mother Superior' when she heard it. She didn't protest. Neither did I.

With my arm tucked firmly under hers, Pat pulled me for the last time through the heavily carved doors with their scenes of earth and of heaven, of heaven and of hell.

"Spiritual!" she snorted.

Chapter 24

We had a big reunion on the Fourth of July—Pearl's birthday. We: Us survivors of the Compton Interregnum.

Pat and I by then had finished roofing the addition to the milking shed. That was easy. Insulating had posed problems. If people found out, they'd know the shed was intended for me not Rosie. The planning board would not like that. In the end I bought the rolls of fiberglass in Greenville and brought them down to Soperton hidden in the trunk of my car.

Pat and I continued to attend the Soperton planning board meetings. That's how we found out that Pearl, Barney and Santa Clara took over the application for that housing sub-division. We already knew the three of them had taken over the temple. There was a long article in the *Ellsworth American* about how it was going to be rededicated to the Virgin of Medjugorje. Why Pat and I went on going to the planning board, though, is a different story.

Suzanne and Pearl were applying for a building permit for a cottage for me out to Shangri-La. When I say cottage, I'm talking Comptonese. Suzanne said she thought five bedrooms would be enough. I said, "Give me a break."

What Pat said, I won't repeat. But she made it clear she expected me to help her block it. Thus our attendance at the planning board. What I hoped was that Barney might want the cottage. She and Santa Clara. But so far, Barney shows no sign of leaving the Cloisters.

With Julie dead, it was easy for Mausinger and the compliant Halifax Police to pin the murders on poor Arthur. They also arranged for him to be settled in the Nova Scotia Hospital with his not-really Grandmother, Anna Maria Zuccollo Compton.

There was one murder I hankered to get set straight: that ancient one of Angus MacDonald, Pearl's father. But I knew it was none of my business. Old Mrs. MacDonald had paid the price, and her wish was for Pearl to be free to make her own amends. And that, in her own fashion, Pearl had done. Corporate charity wasn't to my tastes, but Pearl was right: Shangri-La and H.O.P.E. made a big difference to the local economy. And it's hard to disagree with the proposition that jobs are better than charity.

At that Fourth of July barbecue, late in the evening, after the fireworks, Pearl became very mellow. She reminisced some. Prompted by questions from yours truly. The Zuccollos, in Milan, were Banco D'Ambrosiano bankers. Jacob Compton's early gun-running had recommended him to them, and in the twenties they set Jacob up as their Canadian connection. His natural piety was an asset.

On his seventy-fifth birthday, the Vatican offered him Charles as a personal assistant. It was an offer he couldn't refuse. Literally. When Julie got out of hand, and Jacob became intent on protecting her, Charles slipped easily from his role as assistant into one as warden.

Pearl said to me "I know it's easy to criticize the way Charles handled things. But he held it all together. You have to give him that. All the charities," she explained. "They're all intact."

Bully for the charities!

"I'm not sure," I said, "I understand why you brought Julie back to Halifax with you. What was that all about, leaving her tied up in the bathtub in Suzanne's room?"

Suzanne stuttered sleepily, "I explained that to you Brigid."

"Pearl?" I said.

Pearl busied herself scraping a dish or two, avoiding eye contact. She said, "Charles had some plan." She laughed. The sound was harsh. "There were only so many places we could hold hostages."

"His plan wasn't to have Julie kill me, the better to put the blame on me for the carnage?"

Pearl said, "I expect the planning board will approve the plans for your cottage at the next meeting."

"You must have been some surprised," I replied, "when Julie showed up with the butcher knife."

Pearl turned and looked me full in the eye. "You got that right," she said. "I'd fallen asleep. Did you untie her?"

"Be serious. She was some determined young woman."

"Yes."

"How long had you known about Julie?"

"Known about her?"

"Yeah. Like when I first met her, I thought she was crazy. I didn't appreciate just how crazy, but the stigmata, her saying you planned to kill her, she was very self-centered to say the least. But then everyone seemed to feel sorry for her. When Arthur, who obviously wasn't playing with a full deck, supposedly kidnapped her, I began to pity her, too. It blinded me to the fact that she was the most likely person to have killed Arjuna. They lived together, there was only her word that after she left him to his headache she spent the night sleeping in your office."

"Border line personality disorder."

"Say what?"

"That was the diagnosis."

"You had her diagnosed?"

"Wouldn't you?" Pearl said, dryly. "She *was* my granddaughter."

Somewhere not far away in the woods a whippoorwill began its frenzied, repetitious cry. Suzanne and Pat seemed to have fallen asleep. I decided to ask my last question, the one I didn't want Suzanne to hear, or Pat. I preferred if I could to have my ego battered in private.

"When did you decide to have me take the fall?" I asked.

"I don't understand," said Pearl, obviously lying.

"When did the Old Man realize that Heidi McCarren and I

had once been lovers? When did he assign Suzanne to herd me? To keep me on the case until I was close enough to all of it to be framed?"

Pearl sighed. "He was clever," she said. "And he had a mind for detail. He knew from the start. When Heidi first wrote to him about Eddie, he had her thoroughly researched. Your name came up. He didn't forget it. When I told him what Julie was up to, he said to hire you. He said he'd get Suzanne to keep an eye on you. He said you might be useful later on."

"I thought it was a mighty big coincidence."

Pearl snorted. "The old man, as you call him, never relied on luck."

"Or spiritual laws. You know, if you give it will be returned ten-fold. The charities. They had a firm material basis."

"But of course. He spent his life tending them. They are very sound."

Sounder than some of the people, I thought. Sounder than the good MacDonald women. But I held my tongue.

I thought about those two good women, Faith and Hope. I imagined what it must have been like, Julie's devastating storm of violence that had shattered forever the pastoral setting where I had felt so much peace. Hurricane. Volcano. All the images were natural, vaginal. Mother Nature. Kali. Sweet Julie, veiled, perfumed, erupting. Her aunties might have distrusted her, but they would not have feared Julie.

Still, Julie had moved me too. As unwanted by her father as Eddie had been unwanted by his. But old man Compton had discovered a use for Eddie. No one but Arjuna had found a use for Julie.

Arjuna had made Julie a side show in his carnival. But he had intended to take the show off the road. Except for some bleeding palms, Julie didn't have much going for her. Bloody handprints wouldn't get her far in the Compton line of business, bilking the public in the promotion of charity. It was a line of work that took astuteness, something Pearl had in spades. That the old man had until in old age he mistook the opulence for his own, the power he seemed to wield as something more than borrowed.

Pearl would never end up like James Bakker, in prison, or like the head of United Way, disgraced. She had learned her lessons well. Lessons, clearly, that Julie would not have wanted even to know about.

In the distance, the lake was like glass. The moon shone on its surface, full again as it had been that fateful night when I first visited Scotsburn. The gibber of a loon broke the silence; its frenzied call echoing back from the ridge.

"So!" I said.

"So?" said Pearl. She yawned. It was time to leave.

"It's like Suzanne said, I guess," I added.

"What Suzanne said?"

I toasted Pearl with the dregs of my cream soda. "Long live the Queen."